How My Sister and I Became Superheroes

By Steven Edge

ISBN: 978-1-3650-3977-5 (sc)
ISBN: 978-1-4834-5441-2 (e)

Lulu Publishing Services rev. date: 07/22/2016

Contents

Chapter One

The Beginning

"My name is Danny Steiner and this is my story."

I t all started one rainy afternoon in early July. I was sitting on our living room couch reading a book on my tablet when all of a sudden there was a loud knock at the door. Within a couple of seconds, my little sister, Beth, flew past me like a runaway train that had come off of its tracks and was now out of control. Behind her in hot pursuit, but not quite as fast was my mother. She, too, was just as driven as my sister to answer the door that day.

You see, the problem with my little sister is she can be a bit outspoken at times. In the past, she has been known to leave some lasting impressions on some of the people she meets for the very first time. So my mother always wants to be present whenever she answers the door.

It wasn't long before Beth came running back into the living room at a full gallop. She made it a point to come crashing down right on top of me.

"Beth, get off of me! You're going to break my tablet!"

She quickly stood up and looked at me with this big smile on her face. In her left hand tightly clasped were several strands of white string. These strings were attached to a large bunch of colorful balloons, which were floating above her head.

There she stood just staring at me with this rare silence.

"Ok Beth, I'll bite. Where did you get the balloons?"

"This guy named Steve just gave them to me, and that's not all. He also gave Mom a check for one hundred thousand dollars and keys to a new house."

"No way!"

"Yes way! I cross my heart and hope you die."

"Beth, you've got it backwards. You're supposed to say you die."

"That's what I said, silly."

"Beth, get out of my way! I've got to go check this out for myself."

I was just about to get up from the couch when my mother returned from answering the front door. She, too, was sporting a big smile, accompanied by a spring in her step.

"Mom, is it true what Beth just told me? That some strange man named Steve just handed you a check for one hundred thousand dollars and keys to a new house?"

"It's hard to believe, but it's true," said my mother.

"Did this Steve character tell you the reason for his generosity?"

"Get this, he told me that I won the grand prize drawing from some magazine company which I've never even heard of. I told him that I didn't enter any magazine contest, but I do remember having a magazine subscription a couple of years ago. He told me that must be how they got my name for the grand drawing."

"Wow! This is like the best news ever!"

"I agree." Said my mom. "The only problem is moving to this new house is going to be a big undertaking. In order for this move to go smoothly, the three of us are going to have to work together as a team."

"Not a problem. I will do whatever it takes to help make this move go smoothly."

"Danny, I'm not worried about you doing your share."

My mother then turned and looked over at Beth. My sister just sat there quietly playing with her new balloons.

"I'm going to need your help, too, young lady."

Beth continued to sit there totally ignoring what my mother was saying.

"Beth, please look at me when I'm talking to you."

Beth turned and looked over at my mother with this fake grin on her face.

"Yes, Mother."

"Beth, I'm going to need your help too. I'm also going to need you to be on your best behavior."

Beth's grin quickly turned into a look of disbelief.

"I can't believe what you are saying to me!" Beth cried out. "Do me a favor and look up the word angel in any dictionary. What do you think you'll find? I'll tell you what you'll find! You'll find a picture of me!"

Both my mother and I started laughing. Beth just sat there shaking her head in disbelief.

Within a couple of weeks, the three of us had completed the move into our new house. It turned out that the magazine contest was all a hoax. It was actually a very well organized plan our grandfather had cooked up. A grandfather who we never even knew existed. It seems that the old man was dying and he wanted to meet his grandchildren before he passed away. Since he gave us a brand new house and one hundred thousand dollars, who were we to judge the old geezer.

Chapter Two

The Painting

. . . .

D o you remember Steve from Chapter One? It turns out he works for my grandfather as a live-in caregiver. I know this because they're our new next door neighbors. How convenient is that?

Tonight, we got to meet our grandfather for the very first time over dinner at his house. The dinner itself was uneventful, but what happened afterwards proved to be quite interesting.

While my mother and Steve were in the kitchen washing dishes, Grandpa Jack, Beth and I decided to retire to the living room.

To be respectful, I chose to sit next to my grandfather while Beth sat on the floor playing with Grandpa Jack's twin Labrador puppies, Bonnie and Clyde.

My grandfather was this gray-haired old man, who wheezed whenever he spoke. His wheelchair was his only means of transportation, due to a debilitating disease.

As I sat there scoping out his beautiful house, I noticed this one large painting of an Indian hanging on the wall just above the fireplace.

"Grandpa Jack, where did you get that neat looking Indian painting?" I asked.

All of a sudden, a smile came over his face as his demeanor totally changed. It was as though the fire from his youth had suddenly reignited. He then leaned over toward me and grabbed my arm ever so tightly, while he stared into my eyes. "Danny, I was hoping you would ask me about that painting."

I then realized that his wheezing seemed to have vanished.

"Danny, listen, and listen carefully to what I am about to tell you. It might change yours and your sister's lives forever."

Since my grandfather was old and dying there was no way I could refuse his wishes. So I sat there ever so still, focused on every word that came out of his mouth. I really wasn't expecting any life changing information.

"That is a painting of your great, great grandfather, Shadow Cloud."

With that, Beth stood up and looked directly at the painting. She then spun around and ran directly toward my grandfather, stopping only inches before running into him. She then looked directly into his eyes and shouted out, "Grandpa Jack, that is life changing! Wait until I tell Mom that I'm part Indian! She is going to freak out!"

Within a blink of the eye, Beth went flying out the room. Those two puppies had all they could do to keep up with her grueling pace.

After watching my weird sister bolt out of the room, I turned and looked over at my grandfather.

"I apologize, Grandpa Jack, for my sister's actions."

"Danny, don't ever apologize for your little sister. She's a very gifted individual and someday in the near future, she's going to amaze you beyond belief, mark my words."

I just smiled at my grandfather, thinking he's definitely missing a few cards from his deck.

"Grandpa Jack, is that your life-changing fact that Beth and I are both part Indian?"

"No, don't be silly. Now let me finish my story. There was something very different about your great, great grandfather. He had this very special power."

Suddenly, he stopped talking as though he was waiting for me to react. So to make him happy, I pretended to be excited. "Grandpa Jack, what pray tell was this very special power that my great, great grandfather possessed?"

"Your great, great grandfather had the ability to fly with the hawks, and he was as strong as any full-grown bear, and he could run as fast as the fastest deer."

He said it so seriously that I honestly thought he was joking. So I started laughing.

"Grandpa Jack, are you sure you took all your meds today?"

The second I showed disbelief to his story, the fire in his eyes went out and he started wheezing again.

When I saw how I had affected him, I quickly apologized for my stupid remark, but it was too late. He had already shut down, not uttering another word.

Later on, as we were saying our goodbyes and thanking both Steve and my Grandfather Jack for the lovely dinner, my grandfather decided to speak up one last time.

"Beth and Danny, please do me a big favor. I want you both to take a tour of my animal rescue shelter tomorrow."

Beth was so excited with this new reality that she nearly ripped my mother's arm off.

"Did you hear that, Mom!? My grandfather owns his own animal shelter. Mom, can Danny and I please take a tour of the shelter tomorrow?"

"I don't know, Beth. I've got a lot of shopping to do tomorrow."

Steve quickly spoke up. "I have some business I have to take care at the shelter tomorrow. I would love to take the kids with me and give them a tour of the shelter."

My mother smiled as she looked at the two of us. She then turned and looked back at Steve. "If you're sure it's not an inconvenience, I would really appreciate that."

"How about I pick them up at your house at nine o'clock tomorrow morning?"

"Ok, Steve, we'll see you then."

As the three of us left the house that night, I couldn't help but think what was it my grandfather was about to tell me before I so rudely interrupted him. What did he mean when he said it might be life changing? I was very mad at myself for laughing at him and not getting the whole story. Maybe someday in the near future, I'll be able to get him to finish his story.

Chapter Three

The Animal Shelter

. . . .

As soon as we arrived at the shelter that next morning Steve brought us in to meet Ted. He's the fellow who's responsible for all that goes on at the shelter. When we entered Ted's office, he immediately stood up to greet us.

I was taken aback by the sheer size of the man. He stood nearly seven feet tall and he weighed in excess of three hundred pounds. He was by far the biggest human I'd ever laid eyes on.

Steve quickly introduced us. "Ted, this is Danny and Beth, Jack's grandkids."

First, Ted reached out and shook Beth's hand.

"What a beautiful young lady you are. I bet you are a handful."

Beth looked up at Ted with a smile on her face. "I see you have been reading my bio."

Ted laughed. "It's obvious you're smart too."

Ted then reached out to shake my hand. Seeing his immense size, I realized that my handshake was going to be a lot harder than the one Beth had just experienced.

The second his massive hand clasped my relatively tiny hand, I knew I was right. The pressure he applied to my hand was extreme, to say the least. Even though it hurt quite a bit, I refused to let him see my pain. It was kind of fulfilling to me knowing he wasn't going to show me any mercy due to my youth.

"Danny, you look a lot like your grandfather when he was a much younger man," said Ted.

"I hope that's a compliment, because Beth is always telling me, I'm ugly as sin."

Beth was now having trouble containing her laughter, while Ted reassured me that my grandfather was a good-looking man in those days.

A large box of assorted doughnuts sat on Ted's desk. He quickly spoke up when he saw me eyeing them.

"I wasn't sure if you kids had eaten breakfast yet. So I stopped off at the local bakery on my way in this morning and picked up some doughnuts for us to munch on. So just dig in and grab whatever flavor you desire."

Beth and I had no problem finding our favorite doughnuts. As the four of us sat there eating our doughnuts, I spotted another painting of Shadow Cloud. The pose was different, but the face was unmistakable.

"Ted, I see that you also have a painting of Shadow Cloud on your wall. Last night, my grandfather told me this crazy story about how Shadow Cloud could fly with the hawks, wrestled some bears and he could even outrun a deer."

Ted smiled as he looked over at me.

"Danny, I remember about forty years ago when your grandfather told me that same unbelievable story. I, too, thought it was a bunch of hooey. It took a lot of convincing before I finally came around."

"You actually believe my grandfather's story?"

"Believe it? I lived it through your grandfather for the last forty years."

"How could you have? Shadow Cloud has been dead for a very long time."

"Let me guess. You interrupted your grandfather's story last night?"

"How did you know that? Did my grandfather tell you?"

"No, Danny, he didn't have to. It's obvious you're missing the most important part of that story."

"What's that?" I asked.

"Danny, Shadow Cloud's powers didn't end with his death. His powers still exist today. They were passed down through his bloodline."

That's all it took to light Beth's fuse. She was now ready to show everyone in the room her over-the-top personality. This time she thought standing on a chair would be a good way to get her point across.

"Thank you, Ted! Finally, someone has explained to me what I have known my entire life! I have super powers that no other human being on this planet has!"

Ted laughed out loud.

"Slow down there, young lady. If you actually have these super powers, which I'm not sure you do, you aren't the only one."

"Who else would dare to have my powers?" Beth asked.

"To start with, your grandfather still has his powers. Your father most likely had powers, but refused to use them while he was alive. Last but not least, if you actually do have these powers, there is an excellent chance your brother Danny has them too."

"I've been a super hero for only a couple minutes and I am already sharing the spotlight with others, how depressing."

Beth then climbed down from the chair and returned to her seat. We all laughed, while Beth frowned.

Beth's silence allowed me to continue my conversation with Ted.

"Ted, let's say Beth and I actually have these powers. Neither one of us has enough muscle or body mass to perform such super feats."

"You're absolutely right, Danny. That's why you need a host who has the powers you require."

"What is a host?" I asked.

"Think back to what your grandfather was saying. He told you that Shadow Cloud had great strength, unbelievable speed, and he could fly without wings. In every case he compared Shadow Cloud's power with a specific life form. So here's your answer. A host can be an animal, a bird or a reptile. If the two of you actually possess this power, you will have the ability to transfer your inner being into any one of these living creatures. Once this connection has been made, you will have full control of your host and you will experience everything that your host experiences. We call this power TRANFERANCE."

I couldn't believe what I was hearing.

"Ted, if my calculations are right, then that would mean Beth and I would be able to connect with hundreds of different species."

"Danny, it's more like thousands of species. Think of this, Danny, each one of these creatures has its own unique powers, from the tiny lizard who has the ability to become nearly invisible by altering his skin colors to conform with his surroundings to the mighty elephant who can pull an entire tree out of the ground with his trunk. Danny, these are just two examples. Now multiply this by more than a thousand and you can see that your powers would be almost unlimited."

Beth decided it was time for an encore. Luckily for us she remained seated.

"That means Super Beth has more powers than all the other super heroes put together. Ted, when can Danny and I find out if we actually have these super powers?"

"I can test the both of you right now if you'd like."

Beth was so excited she stuffed almost an entire doughnut into her mouth and then mumbled, "I'm ready!"

The three of us got up and left the room, while Steve stayed behind attempting to polish off the remaining doughnuts.

Chapter Four

The Test

. . . .

There we were, the three of us, just standing there staring at this strange looking test chamber. It's the same chamber that will soon determine if Beth and I possess the power of our ancestors. To us, it wasn't just a stationary object, but instead a possible vehicle that may soon transport the two of us to a new reality with new adventures.

Prior to starting the experiment, Ted attached numerous sensors to both of our heads. Once the sensors were in place, it was now time for us to enter the chamber. Since I was the biggest, it only made sense that I would enter the chamber first.

As soon as I was seated inside the chamber, I realized there was something very wrong. It felt as though the walls of the chamber were closing in on me. In addition to that, I started experiencing shortness of breath. I knew the only way I was going to get through this experiment was to somehow convince myself that the inside of this chamber was much larger than it actually was.

Now it was Beth's turn to enter the chamber. Prior to climbing inside, Beth decided to poke her head inside the hatch so she could check out the seating arrangements. She wasn't impressed to say the least. "I specifically remember asking my travel agent for first-class seating. This looks a lot like coach to me!"

Then Beth looked directly at me. "Oh, my God! What's wrong with you, big brother?"

"I not sure, but I think I'm claustrophobic."

"Oh, Ted! Mr. Flight Attendant! We have a sick passenger in seat 1A. He thinks he's claustrophobic."

Ted came running over and took one look at me.

"This isn't good! Danny, do you think you will be able to go through with this experiment?"

"Don't worry, I'll get through it."

Ted then motioned to Beth for her to enter the chamber, and that is exactly what she did. The only problem was, instead of being considerate about my condition, she chose to climb right in on top of me. "Move over, Danny, and stop breathing so hard. You're using up all the oxygen!" She then started laughing uncontrollably.

"Beth, you're not funny!"

Suddenly the lights went out in the chamber and at the same time Ted's voice came blaring out over a speaker that I was sitting on. Beth and I both nearly jumped out of our skins.

"Listen up! Your destination today will be your grandfather's backyard. Danny, your host animal will be Clyde your grandfather's male Labrador puppy. Beth, your host animal will be Bonnie your grandfather's female Labrador puppy. Are there any questions before I throw the switch?"

Fearing that we might injure the puppies, I asked Ted numerous questions concerning their health. He assured me that no harm would come to the dogs.

"One last thing before I throw this switch, keep an eye out for your grandfather. He will be visiting you at the test site today. If there are no further questions, I will now commence the countdown. Ten, nine, eight..."

Beth quickly interrupted Ted's countdown. "Hold on, Ted! Before you throw that switch, you've got to tell me what it's going to feel like?"

"I was hoping you weren't going to ask that question. According to your grandfather, it's going to feel like you're falling off a cliff."

With that one fact, Beth began to freak out.

"I'm too young to die! Maybe I'm not cut out to be a superhero! I should just be satisfied with being a brilliant, attractive young lady!"

Ted then attempted to calm Beth down with some logic. "Beth, you're not going to die! Your grandfather has done this thousands of times and he's still alive."

Being in such close proximity to my sister, I could tell it was only going to be a matter of seconds before she was going to bail on us. I knew I had to come up with something really fast.

"Beth, do you remember last night when you ran out of the room to tell Mom you were part Indian?"

"Yeah, I remember!"

"While you were out of the room, Grandpa Jack told me that you're a very gifted individual. He also said that someday in the near future you are going to amaze me beyond belief."

That was exactly what Beth needed to hear. Her fear of falling was gone and her confidence had returned.

"I always said Grandpa Jack had an eye for talent," said Beth. "So let's not let the old man down. Ted, forget the countdown. Just throw the darn switch!"

Ted didn't hesitate to throw that switch that day. The last thing I remember before leaving the animal shelter was Beth screaming out the words, "Holy Crap!"

Chapter Five

Grandpa Jack's Backyard

T he second Ted threw the switch, I felt my inner consciousness being drawn out of my body and then lifted up and out through the shelter's roof. Once outside the shelter, I continued to climb higher and higher, until I was just about to enter the clouds.

Then like a meteor caught in the earth's gravitational field, I was dragged back down towards earth at an unbelievable speed. Suddenly, everything came to a complete stop, and I found myself in total darkness.

When I finally opened my eyes, I knew right away something was very different. My relatively small human nose was now gone. My field of vision was now being impaired by a much larger nose. This larger nose was covered with thick dark fur.

It was at that moment in time that I realized the test was a complete success.

It was now time for me to locate Bonnie, Grandpa Jack's other puppy. So I slowly turned Clyde around so I could see behind him. Just as I suspected, Bonnie was sitting behind Clyde. I now had to determine if Beth had successfully completed her transference. Since dogs can't talk, I decided to lift up one of my paws and wave at her. I was totally amazed at the response that followed.

"What took you so long, Danny!?"

I was so thrilled when I heard Beth's voice, I couldn't restrain myself. I ran right over to her and licked her right in her face.

"Danny! Get a hold of yourself! You act like we've been apart for a very long period of time. It's only been a few minutes."

"Beth, how is it I can hear every word that you are saying? Why aren't your lips moving? What am I saying? Dogs can't talk!"

"Don't ask me! Ask Grandpa Jack when he gets here."

"That's a good idea."

All of a sudden, Beth went running toward the far corner of the fence that was adjacent to our property. "Danny, come here and look. It's Mom! She's getting into the car to go shopping. I'm going to get her to come over here."

"Beth you're wasting your time."

"Mom, look over here! It's me, Beth, your daughter. Look, Mom, Danny and I have turned into these cute little puppies. Don't you want come over and pet us?"

Beth then turned around and looked at me. "I can't believe it! Mom looked directly at us and then she had the nerve to get into her car and drive away."

"Beth, the only thing she heard was you barking. Then when she turned and looked, all she saw was Bonnie and Clyde, Grandpa Jack's two labrador puppies. There was no way she could have known it was us."

All of a sudden a large shadow passed right over both of us.

"Beth, did you see that?"

"If you're talking about the shadow, then, yes I saw it. What's the big deal? It probably was just an airplane or something."

While Beth continued to blab, I quickly spotted the culprit. There perched on top of my Grandpa Jack's picnic table was this very large hawk. It seemed to be extremely interested in both me and Beth. Or, should I say, Grandpa Jack's twin Labrador puppies.

"Beth, do me a favor and look over there at Grandpa Jack's picnic table."

Beth spun Bonnie around so she could see what I was staring at. "Wow, that is one beautiful bird!" Beth exclaimed.

I couldn't for the life of me understand why Beth wasn't freaking out right about now. "It's a hawk, Beth! Hawks eat small animals. Hawks have been known on occasion to kill and eat small dogs."

Beth came running over toward me for protection. "Danny, what are we going to do?!"

"I have an idea, we'll both lie down and play dead and maybe the hawk will fly away."

Beth protested, "It's too late for that! He's already seen us walking around!"

"Listen to me, Beth. There is no way we can outrun that hawk, and we definitely can't outfight him. So playing dead is our only option."

"Ok, I'll go first," Beth said.

Beth started her act by pretending she was choking. She then followed it up with a graceful fall to the ground. She ended it with this one last gasp for air before succumbing to her early demise. It looked so convincing, that I decided to do the exact same thing, right down to the last gasp of air.

We both laid there totally still for several minutes before the hawk took flight. Too bad for us, he didn't fly away. Instead he landed only a couple of inches away from where we were lying down. Then something really amazing happened: the hawk started talking!

"You two clowns would be a lot more convincing if you would just keep your eyes closed."

"Danny!" Beth said. "The hawk is absolutely right! We must keep our eyes closed (no more peeking)."

"Beth, are you listening to what you're saying?"

Again the hawk spoke. "Danny James Steiner, I have one question and only one question for you."

How could this bird know my name? My curiosity soon got the best of me, so I asked, "What is your question?"

"Danny Steiner, did you remember to take your meds today?"

I couldn't believe it! My dying old grandfather has just paid me back with interest for the stupid remark that I made the night before.

I quickly sat up and looked directly at my grandfather, the hawk.

In fear for her life, Beth whispered, "Danny, lie back down. You're going to get us both killed."

"Beth, get up and say hello to your grandfather."

Beth jumped up, wagging her tail and got right up into the hawk's face. "Grandpa Jack, you are one bad looking super hero! I'm damn glad you're on our side!"

After hearing Beth's remark, Grandpa Jack couldn't help but laugh. Accompanying my grandfather's laugh was that same familiar wheezing that I'd heard from the night before.

"Grandpa Jack, how is it we are all talking to each other and none of us are moving our lips or in your case, your beak?"

"Danny, when our conscious beings leave our bodies, our bodies automatically enter into a subconscious state. Even though our conscious beings are presently located here inside our host animals we are still very much connected with our human bodies. So when Beth talks, her human body says what she is saying. Danny, since you're sitting next to Beth in the chamber you hear exactly what she says. Even though these conversations are being held quite a long distance away, to us it sounds like we are talking to each other right here and right now."

Beth then asked a question. "If that's the case, then how are we communicating with you? Did you climb inside the chamber with us?"

"No, don't be silly. I could never fit in the chamber with the two of you. My old chamber was designed for only one person. Since you two are still young, we knew we could squeeze the two of you in together. So here is the answer to your question. My human body is presently located in my other transference chamber, which is located inside my house. The reason why we can all communicate with each other is easy. I had Ted electronically connect the two chambers so we could talk to each other."

"Grandpa Jack, is there anything else we should know when we do these transfers?" asked Beth.

"Yes, there are three rules you two need to follow. Rule number one: never put your host animal in harm's way. Rule number two: don't ever use your powers to commit a crime. Last but not least, you can't tell anyone about your newfound powers."

Beth raised her paw. "Can we tell our mother?"

"Nope, you can't even tell your mother."

Then grandfather asked, "Are there any other questions before Ted returns you back to your human bodies?"

I couldn't let my grandfather leave without asking him this one last question. "Grandpa Jack, my experience connecting with Clyde was quite scary. Is it always going to be like that?"

"No, the closer you are to your host animal during your transfer, the less extreme your experience will be. If you're in the same room as your host animal during your transfer, you won't feel a thing."

"So why didn't Ted bring the puppies to the animal shelter to make it easier on us?"

"Ted and I both decided to make the test hard so we could prepare you two for a worst-case situation. In the future you two most likely will never have to make a transfer over such a great distance again, but if you do, you'll both be ready."

"I must remember to thank Ted when I get back," said Beth.

"It's time for us to end this first training session," said my grandfather. "It was really great seeing you two kids in action, especially Beth's Oscar-winning death scene performance. I love you both, and remember everything that I've told you." With that my Grandpa Jack's hawk rocketed up into the sky with very little effort.

"Danny, did you hear what Grandpa Jack said? He said my death scene was an Oscar winning performance. I told you that he had an eye for talent."

All of a sudden, Ted's voice came from nowhere. "Are you two ready come back yet?"

When I heard Ted's voice I couldn't believe it. "Ted, were you able to communicate with us this whole time?"

"Yup, I told you I was going to monitor the test."

"Why didn't you tell us Grandpa Jack was the hawk?"

"We needed to see how you two could perform in a difficult situation."

"So how did we do?"

"I would say you both passed with flying colors."

Beth interrupted Ted. "If you two are done talking I would like to take my tour of the shelter now."

With that Ted decided to throw the switch again without warning. The trip back wasn't quite as scary, because this time I was aware of what was going to happen.

After returning, Steve gave Beth and me the grand tour of the shelter.

Today was definitely the most memorable day of my life. I can't even imagine what our future has in store for us. There was one thing I was sure of. Our lives would never be the same again.

Chapter Six

A New Family Member

B eth spent the better part of the afternoon filling my mother in on all aspects of our day at the shelter. Amazingly, she was able to avoid any discussion that might hinge upon our newly discovered powers.

It's now 6 p.m. at the Steiner house, and we had just finished eating dinner. Thinking that my mother had heard all that she wanted to hear about today's activities, I was totally blown away when she asked me this one specific question.

"Danny, is there something that happened this morning at the shelter that Beth isn't telling me about?"

My mother's question left me speechless. I sat there trying to keep my composure, while my mother just stared at me. Finally, it came to me, an answer that would suffice and at the same time protect the integrity of our secret.

"There was this one thing Beth didn't tell you about."

This really got my mother's full attention. Beth on the other hand was not impressed. She even went so far as to call out my name. "Danny!"

"What is it that Beth didn't tell me?" my mother asked.

"I bet you anything that Beth didn't tell you about us touring the reptile room."

You could tell by the look on my mother's face, that wasn't the answer she was looking for.

"You're right. Beth never mentioned the reptile room. Think hard, was there any one specific animal that you two might have seen that caught your interest?"

"That's easy," said Beth. "There was this one cute little Labrador puppy named Scruffy. It turns out he's Bonnie and Clyde's little brother."

You could tell by the smile on my mother's face that this was the answer she had been waiting for.

My mother then stood up from the kitchen table and walked over to the basement door and opened it. All of a sudden, that same little black Labrador puppy that we had just been talking about came running into the kitchen wagging his tail and jumping all over me and Beth.

Beth and I sat there totally confused. You see, neither Beth nor I had ever had a pet in our entire lives. Our father wouldn't allow it.

"Your grandfather called me this morning while you two were at the shelter," said my mom. He asked me if it would be OK if he gave you two a puppy. Come to find out, that was one of the reasons why they brought you to the shelter this morning, it was to see if you two would take a liking to one of the animals. The word got back to your grandfather that Scruffy was the animal that the both of you showed the most interest in."

"So, after listening to what your grandfather had to say, I told him that I couldn't think of a better way to reward you two for all the hard work that you did to ensure that our move to this new house went so smoothly."

Beth sprang up out of her seat and ran over and hugged my mother. "Thank you, Mom! You're the best! Can I please pick up the puppy?"

"Don't ask me. Ask yourself. He's your puppy."

Beth ran over and scooped Scruffy up off of the floor and started showering him with kisses.

"I want you two to take Scruffy into the other room and play with him, while I clean up in here," said my mom.

She didn't have to tell us twice. Beth went running from the room in her same lunatic fashion, while I chose to exit like a civil human being.

Chapter Seven

The Home Experiment

. . . .

I was on my way into the living room when something occurred to me. Could it be possible that our grandfather gave Scruffy to us so that we could practice our newfound powers at home? There was only one problem with my reasoning. Without a test chamber it would be futile -- or would it? There was one way I could find out. I would have to attempt a transfer using Scruffy as my test subject. Knowing that Beth would be less than enthusiastic about me using her dog as a guinea pig, I decided to keep her in the dark for now.

In the living room, I discovered Beth sitting on the floor attempting to teach Scruffy a bunch of new tricks. She was so focused on what she was doing; she didn't realize that I was standing there watching her. This was the perfect time for me to attempt my transfer.

To keep Beth from seeing what I was about to do, I decided to take cover behind the couch.

As soon as I was in position, I closed my eyes and pictured Scruffy in my mind. The transfer was so uneventful I honestly thought that it hadn't taken place. Then when I opened my eyes, I found myself standing next to a much larger and scarier version of my baby sister. I soon realized that she only appeared that way, because I was staring at her through Scruffy's eyes.

It was now time for me and Scruffy to go to work. Beth had been barking out commands to Scruffy for the last several minutes and now she was just sitting there staring at the ceiling. You could tell that she had given up on Scruffy's training session for the night.

So to get her attention, I had Scruffy bark several times in her direction. She quickly responded, "What's up, Scruffy? Was I ignoring you?"

"Woof, woof!" Scruffy and I said.

"I'm sorry I ignored you, Scruffy."

Normally I wouldn't mess with Beth's head, but with the anonymity that came with this situation, I couldn't help myself. So without any direction from Beth, I decided that Scruffy and I would attempt a series of tricks.

We started with a single rollover to the right. We then followed that up with our famous begging pose, and last but not least, a good old-fashioned handshake for an ending.

Our performance went so smoothly that tears started flowing from Beth's eyes. Her reaction was priceless.

"Scruffy, I knew you could do it!" said Beth.

As a reward for our great performance, Beth decided to pick us up and kiss us on our noses.

Then something bad happened. She was just about to put us back down when she hesitated. At first, I didn't think much about it. Then suddenly, I realized her demeanor had totally changed, I knew right then that I was in trouble.

"Danny James Steiner! What are you doing inside Scruffy?! I don't know how you did it, but I'll give you ten seconds to get out.

If you're not out in ten seconds, I'm coming in after you and I'm going to drag you out."

The fear of our two brains sharing the same space at the same time was too much for me to handle. So I quickly disconnected from Scruffy and stood up from behind the couch and unconditionally surrendered.

Beth was so amused with my instantaneous surrender that she started laughing.

"What's the matter, big brother? The thought of us being in the same host animal at the same time scare you? It's a good thing you surrendered when you did. You probably would have needed professional help to regain your sanity after I got done with you."

"That's really funny, Beth, but I must admit the thought did cross my mind."

"So Danny, how did you do it?"

"Do what?"

"How did you connect with Scruffy without using Grandpa Jack's chamber?"

"All I did was close my eyes and picture Scruffy in my mind at the same time."

Beth then closed her eyes and within a couple of seconds, Scruffy was preforming a series of new tricks. Some of these tricks I'd never even seen before. Then Beth opened her eyes and looked at me.

"Danny, I think we should call Grandpa Jack and tell him about our discovery."

"Beth, I think he already knows."

"If that is the case, where do we go from here?"

"I think it's time we visit the zoo!"

Right then my mother walked into the room.

"That's a great idea, Danny. What do you think, Beth? Would you like to go to the zoo with me and Danny tomorrow?"

"I would love to go to the zoo tomorrow," said Beth.

"OK, it's a date. Now Danny, go downstairs to the basement and you'll find a large cage for Scruffy to sleep in. Beth, I need you to go in the linen closet and grab a blanket for Scruffy to sleep on as well."

As Beth and I exited the room, we could hardly contain ourselves. I don't think either one of us got much sleep that night.

Chapter Eight

A Day at the Zoo

. . . .

While we were driving to the zoo that next morning, Beth wouldn't stop talking about the time the three of us visited this small petting zoo. According to Beth, it was one of the most memorable days of her life.

All I can remember from that day was the pungent smell that accompanied those same farm animals.

After listening to Beth's petting zoo story for the umpteenth time, both my mother and I had heard enough. So out of pure desperation, my mother made Beth this promise.

"Beth, as soon we arrive at the zoo, the three of us will go find some farm animals and we'll pet them."

Beth responded with an enthusiastic "Yes!"

Once we got to the zoo, my mother inquired about the possibility of us petting some farm animals during our visit. We were told by one of the zoo employees that the petting portion of their zoo had been closed several years earlier, due to legal reasons. Beth wasn't at all happy with this employee's answer. Right away, I could see her eyes welling up with tears. I quickly pointed it out to my mother hoping that she could prevent Beth's pending meltdown, but it was too late. Beth then fell to the ground bawling her eyes out. Then out of nowhere this young man walked over and whispered something into Beth's ear. Suddenly, Beth stood up and wiped the tears from her eyes and then looked at us like nothing had happened. Most people would have been taken aback by Beth's strange behavior, but it didn't faze me or my mother one bit. We've gotten used to Beth's strange behavior over the years.

Beth then told us that the young man who had just whispered into her ear was an employee of the zoo and he had just invited the three of us to go along with him to feed a small herd of hungry goats. Of course we took him up on his invitation.

So there we were, the four of us standing amongst what we thought was a small herd of hungry goats in this very large fenced in area. At one end of the enclosure, my mother and the young man stood talking to each other, while at the other end Beth and I were attempting to feed all of these hungry goats.

When we first started feeding the goats everything seemed to be working out just fine. Then something happened. The small number of goats that we had originally started with had soon swelled into a much larger number of goats.

Then I saw one of the goats that I'd been feeding running directly towards Beth. We will never know why he did what he did that day, but I will never forget what he ended up doing when he got there. I'm guessing the little guy just wanted to get Beth's attention, because as soon as he got next to Beth he decided to head butt Beth right in her rear end.

It was quite a funny sight, I must admit. I couldn't help but laugh. That was until Beth turned and looked directly at me with one of her insane stares. I knew right away I was going to pay for the goat's misdeeds.

"Danny James Steiner, how dare you head butt your own sister."

"Beth, I swear I didn't do it! It was the goat; he did it all on his own!"

"Likely story! Danny, how fast do you think you can run?"

"Let me guess, I hope I can outrun a goat."

Beth then closed her eyes and that same little goat that had just got done head butting her was now headed in my direction. I quickly dropped my bucket of oats and started running in the opposite direction. Luckily for me, it was the same direction in which my mother and the young man were standing. I was hoping that Beth would call off the attack as soon as I got in the vicinity of my mother, but I was wrong. This is when I felt the goat's teeth latch on to my pants. I knew if I didn't do something really fast my buttocks was next. So I did what any other kid would do who feared for his life.

"Mom, help me!"

My call for help worked. The goat quickly let go of my pants and he stopped his pursuit.

"Danny, what did you do to that goat to get him so mad at you?" my mother asked.

"Don't ask me. Ask your daughter, it's all her fault."

My mother then turned and looked over at my sister.

"Don't look at me," said Beth. "I'm just standing here minding my own business feeding these cute little goats."

We left that goat enclosure shortly after my close encounter with death.

The next stop on our tour was this large brick building they called the bird house. Just outside the building was this large sign that indicated there would be a bird show starting in about twenty minutes. So we decided to go inside and check it out.

Once inside the building, we realized that the previous show was still in progress. The room in which the show was taking place was packed. Since there were numerous other birds in other cages in an adjacent room we decided we would go check them out instead. My mother made a beeline towards this one cage that contained these two colorful parrots. As soon as my mother got next to the cage, one of the parrots climbed down off its perch to greet her. She was so impressed with this bird's desire to make friends with her, she decided to talk to him. "Hi there, Mr. Parrot."

That bird didn't utter a word.

All of a sudden, I felt a tug on my shirt. I turned and saw Beth signaling to me to take control of the parrot. I smiled at her and nodded my head in agreement.

I then turned back toward my mother and closed my eyes. Within a second or two, I had taken full control of the parrot. I then waited patiently, hoping that my mother would say something else to the parrot so I could strike up a conversation with her. I didn't have to wait long.

"What is your name?" My mother asked the parrot.

"My name? My name is Poopy Caca," the parrot answered.

All three of us started laughing at the parrot's response. It was even better than I could have imagined. The parrot's voice sounded nothing like my own voice. There was no way my mother could have connected the parrot's response with my own.

Then my mother said, "Hold everything! Parrots can't talk in complete sentences. They're not that smart."

Beth took this as an invitation to join the conversation. So she quickly connected with the other parrot in the cage and said the following.

"I'll have you know, lady, I graduated top of my class at Yale University."

"If you went to Yale," asked my mother, "what did you major in?"

"English grammar, of course."

This is when my mother started acting really weird. First she bent down and looked under the cage. Then she started walking around the cage. She even went as far as to bang on the cage.

I quickly grabbed my sister's arm and shook her so she would disconnect from the parrot that she was controlling.

"Mom, what are you doing?" I asked.

"I'm looking for either a camera or a microphone or something of that nature. There has to be one around here somewhere. Maybe they hid it inside the cage with the parrots."

My mother then attempted to remove the lock that had been placed on the cage door to prevent people from messing with the birds.

I now had two good reasons to let my mother off of the hook. The first reason was she was acting really strange. The second reason was the bird show in the adjacent room was just letting out and there were a lot of people headed our way. So this is what I had my parrot say.

"This is Bob Clark; host of 'We're Just Messing with You TV'. I would like to thank the three of you for talking with us today. If this show ever gets picked up by one of the networks in the future, we will contact you for your permission to air this segment."

Just like always, Beth had to add her two cents in by having her parrot get the last word.

"This is Jane Marks, Bob's co-host. I've got to tell you before you leave. Even though your son is a hideous-looking creature, your daughter is quite beautiful. I highly recommend that you send her to modeling school as soon as possible. Have a nice day and we hope we'll see you all again, real soon."

Once my mother believed it was a TV show experiment, she regained her composure and started acting normal again.

The final stop on our tour of the zoo was the primate section. By the size of the crowd, I could tell it was the biggest draw at the park.

Luckily for us, we got there just in time to watch the show. There, standing on this makeshift stage, stood an animal trainer and these two chimpanzees. The first thing the trainer did was to introduce the crowd to these two adorable looking chimps named Bosco and Bernie. He then sat them down on two wooden stools that had been placed on the stage earlier. In front of each chimp was a canvas, some brushes and a pallet with several colors of paint smeared on them.

I whispered to Beth that I would take control of Bosco if she would take control of Bernie.

She agreed to my terms.

The trainer then told the two chimps to start painting. Both Beth and I had the exact same idea. Instead of painting some funky looking abstract picture, we decided to write something instead. Within a couple of minutes, we were both done.

The trainer remained seated for several more minutes before he finally got up to check their artwork. Then he just stood there staring at the two canvasses with his mouth wide open. The man was in shock. He finally snapped out of it, looked back at the audience and said the following.

"I can't even attempt to explain to all of you what just happened. What I will do is let you see the results for yourselves."

He then held up both canvasses for all to see. On my canvas I had written (E=MC squared) Einstein's theory of relativity. On Beth's canvas she had written "Apes are people too".

The entire crowd was awed by Beth's and my artwork. There were all kinds of responses. Some people laughed while others just stood there in shock. One lady even screamed out, "The end is near!"

This was the straw that broke the camel's back. My mother had seen enough, so she grabbed both Beth's and my hands and literally dragged us to the nearest exit.

My mother didn't say a single word to us on our way back home that day. I realize now that we had goon too fare.

Chapter Nine

The Unexpected Visitor

I was lying on my bed watching TV, when all of a sudden Beth came barging into my room.

"Danny, there's someone outside my bedroom window trying to break in!"

"Beth, go back to sleep! You probably had a bad dream."

"I know it wasn't a dream, because I hadn't gone to sleep yet! Danny, you're always saying that you're the man of the house, it's time you prove it!"

"Beth, you better not be pulling my leg!"

Reluctantly, I climbed out of bed and grabbed a golf club from behind my bedroom door that I'd been saving for a situation just like this.

With my trusty golf club in my right hand and Beth by my side, the two of us made our way back down the hallway toward Beth's room.

As soon as I got to Beth's door, I opened it to discover that her room was shrouded in total darkness. Normally, I wouldn't think twice about entering a darkened room, but the possibility of meeting up with a prowler made the situation a whole lot scarier.

Beth's bedroom has only one light source, a small lamp located in the same vicinity as the window in question.

"Beth, I have an idea," I whispered. "We'll both go in together."

"Danny, I'll go in with you under one condition," said Beth. "You let me carry the golf club."

I knew I couldn't do it alone, so I reluctantly handed Beth my seven iron. As I stood there watching my little sister take several practice swings with my club, I realized I had something new to worry about, the possibility that my own little sister might mistake me for the prowler and beat the crap out of me with my own club. "Beth, before you start swinging that club, you've got to verify your target."

"Danny, are you afraid that I'm going to mistake you for the prowler?"

"Yes, that is exactly what I'm afraid of. Now let's get this over with before Mom gets involved."

I entered the room first, while Beth followed close behind. Slowly we made our way toward Beth's bedroom window, being as quiet as possible. When we finally got to the window, I noticed that the curtains were closed making it impossible for us to see who or what was lurking outside. I was just about to pull open the curtains when all of a sudden we heard a loud tapping noise coming from just outside of the window. Beth panicked and accidently whacked me on the head with my own golf club as she went running out of the room. Holding my head with my right hand, I reached over with my left hand and turned on Beth's light. Then without hesitation, I quickly pulled the curtains back to reveal the culprit. There sitting just outside the window was this little creature. He couldn't have been much more than a foot tall.

"Beth, come here. You've got to see this for yourself."

Beth had no problem reentering the room knowing that the light was on and the coast was clear. She walked straight over to her window and looked out. "Danny! Why is there an owl sitting outside my window?"

"I don't know, but let's find out."

Beth then backed away from the window in preparation for the owl's arrival. I unlocked the window with one hand and opened it with the other. As soon as the window was open, the owl flew into the room and made one complete lap around the room before finally landing on Beth's bed. Thinking that the owl might be connected with my grandfather. I decided to ask him this one question.

"Are you my grandfather?"

The owl responded, "Whoooo, whoooo!"

Beth and I couldn't help but laugh.

So I then asked the owl a different question. "What is it that you want, Mister Owl?"

I could tell right away that owl knew exactly what I was saying, because without hesitation he stretched out one of his claws towards me and in that claw was the smallest cell phone that I had ever seen. He then dropped the cell phone on the bed just in front of me. As soon as it hit the bed it started ringing. So I quickly picked it up and answered it. It was my grandfather just as I suspected. He then asked me to put the phone on speaker mode so he could talk to both of us at the same time. So I did.

"How are my favorite two grandchildren doing tonight?"

I responded, "We were doing just fine until you scared us half to death."

"I'm sorry for scaring you two, but it was important that I talk to both of you tonight."

Beth then asked, "Where's your hawk, Grandpa Jack?"

"He's sleeping in a tree just outside my bedroom window. I chose to use my owl instead, because of his ability to see in the dark."

I quickly changed the subject. "Grandpa Jack, what is it you wanted to talk to us about?"

"I was watching the ten o'clock news tonight, when all of a sudden a special report came on. According to this reporter, there were two very talented chimpanzees who did something really amazing at the zoo today. Does either one of you know what these two chimps did?"

Beth and I just stood there speechless.

"I guess I'll have to tell you," said my grandfather. "One of the chimps wrote the words 'Chimps are people too,' while the other chimp went a whole lot further and wrote down Einstein's theory of relativity. So here is my question to you two. Did you, enjoy your trip to the zoo today?"

"Yes we did, Grandpa Jack!" said Beth. "Danny and I had a great time."

"I must admit; it was quite impressive what you two did. The only problem is; people fear the unknown. So I'm here tonight to ask you to keep a low profile when it comes to using your powers out in public. You don't want to draw attention to yourselves."

Beth and I both agreed to limit the use of our powers when out in public for now on.

"Something else you two need to be aware of," Grandpa Jack added. "There are a lot of bad people in this world who wouldn't hesitate to kidnap both of you for your powers. So keep an eye out for any strangers acting unusual."

"What should we do if we encounter a situation like that?" I asked.

"You can contact me and I'll come and help you, or a better solution is you two join forces and take care of the problem on your own."

At the end of conversation with our grandfather, we said our goodbyes and thanked him for educating us on our new powers. Grandpa Jack's owl then exited the room in the same fashion that he had entered it, through Beth's bedroom window.

Chapter Ten

The Dog Park

. . . .

The next morning Beth and I decided that we would take Scruffy to the local dog park.

When we arrived at the park we were amazed by its sheer size. We were even more amazed by the number of dogs and dog owners that were using the park that day.

As we made our way around the park, Beth and I made it a point to greet everyone we came in contact with.

Scruffy on the other hand was much more interested in the dogs than their owners. I was really impressed at how many friends Scruffy made that day.

After being on our feet for the better part of the morning, we decided it was time for us to take a break.

"Look, Danny!" said Beth. "There's a bench we can sit on."

As we sat quietly on the bench resting our feet, we found ourselves becoming mesmerized by a young couple playing Frisbee with their dog. What we didn't realize at the time was that Scruffy had just slipped out of his collar and was running free and unattended.

If it wasn't for a young girl screaming at the top of her lungs, we probably would've lost Scruffy that day.

The second I heard that blood curdling scream, I turned and saw Scruffy being pinned down on the ground by what I can only describe as the largest German shepherd I had ever seen in my entire life. There was no way I could have gotten over there in time to save Scruffy's life. So I did the only thing I could do. I closed my eyes and immediately attempted a transfer with the giant beast who was trying to kill my dog.

Something must have gone wrong during my transfer, because once inside the dog's head I couldn't see, hear or smell a thing. The only thing I was sure of was that I had total control of the creature's entire body.

Knowing that Scruffy's life was in immediate danger, I chose to drop the unruly beast to the ground like a sack of potatoes. I waited patiently in total darkness unaware of what was going on around me. Without knowing Scruffy's status I had no other option, but to restrain the beast. As the seconds turned into minutes my patience began to run out.

Then the unexpected happened. I heard Beth's voice, not coming from outside, but coming from within the creature's body. I don't think I have to tell you how much this freaked me out.

"Danny, it's amazing whom you bump into when you're making an unscheduled transfer. We must have transferred into the killer dog at the exact same time."

"Beth, let me guess, you can see and hear everything happening around us? If that is the case, please do me a favor and tell me what's going on."

"Now let's see, the good news is Scruffy is alive and well and hiding under the same bench where we are still sitting. The bad news is the owner of this giant pooch thinks her dog was shot, because of the way you dropped him to the ground. She's presently hugging her dying dog and crying uncontrollably."

"Beth, on the count of three we'll both disconnect at the same time. One, two, three!"

When I finally opened my eyes, I saw Beth placing Scruffy's collar back around his neck and adjusting it to ensure we didn't have a repeat performance.

"Danny, how does it feel to know you've just shared a brain with your demented baby sister?" said Beth.

"I must admit it wasn't as bad as I thought it would be."

"Just wait until your brain starts absorbing some of the material that I downloaded into it."

I didn't want to tell her that it was already happening.

After that day I started asking myself some really strange questions. For example, "Am I as pretty as I think I am? What kind of man will I marry? How would I look in a pair of really tight jeans?"

My new desires included world domination, winning the Miss America pageant and being knighted by the Queen of England.

The only good thing that came from my close encounter of the stranger kind was I now have a better understanding of my baby sister and hopefully she of me. I wouldn't trade Beth for a million dollars. Maybe two! Ha, ha.

Chapter Eleven

The Stranger

. . . .

After our exciting day at the dog park, Beth, Scruffy and I were now quietly sitting on our porch watching a flock of robins feverishly searching for worms on our front lawn. All was right at the Steiner house. At least that is what we thought.

Suddenly, I heard the front door open behind me. I turned to see my mother standing in our doorway holding a plate of freshly baked cookies. I smiled at her, but for some reason she didn't smile back. In fact, she wasn't even paying any attention to me.

"Mom, what's up?" I asked.

"It seems we have a Peeping Tom in our midst," my mother said.

"I don't think I know anybody named Tom," said Beth. "He must be new to our neighborhood."

I quickly stood up so I could see whom my mother was talking about. From a standing position, I had no problem spotting the middle-aged man who was sitting inside his car spying on us with a pair of binoculars.

Right away, I recognized the fellow from the old beat up car that he was driving. It was the same guy who stopped me and Beth this morning to ask us for directions. I kind of thought it was weird that the stranger was asking for directions to the exact same street that we lived on. Not realizing that the guy had bad intentions, I gave him the directions and he drove away. I didn't think any more about it until now.

My mother handed me the plate of cookies and retreated back into the house threatening to call the police.

"Danny, what's going on?" asked Beth.

"Stay seated and I'll tell you."

I then placed the plate of cookies on the small table right in front of where Beth was sitting and returned to my seat.

"Beth, do you remember that guy who stopped us this morning at the dog park and asked us for directions?"

"Yeah, I remember him. He's the guy who was driving that crappy old car."

"It seems that same guy is at this very moment parked across the street from our house sitting in his car, and staring at us through a pair of binoculars."

"This is exactly what Grandpa Jack warned us about," said Beth, her voice tinged with apprehension, "What are we going to do now, Danny?"

I sat there for a couple of minutes trying to come up with a plan and then it came to me.

"Beth, I have an idea, it will require us to work together at a speed that might be unattainable. It will also require us to make a substantial number of transfers in a matter of seconds, while at the same time we will be performing a series of aerial maneuvers that would scare even the most seasoned pilot. Are you up for this challenge?"

"It's obvious to me that you're planning on using the robins to do your dirty work. I just don't understand how?"

"Beth, we're going to bomb this guy and his car with bird poop."

Beth's face lit up. "I must admit I like your choice of weapons. My only question is: how do you plan on getting this guy, let's call him Tom for now, to come out of his car so we can bomb him with bird poop?"

"Leave that up to me. Now while I'm getting him to come out of his car, I need you somehow to relocate this entire flock of robins into the old oak tree across the street just prior to our attack. Do you think you can pull that off?"

Beth gave a crisp salute. "General Steiner, I will have all of our troops relocated up in the old oak tree and standing by for further orders by the time you get creepy Tom out of his car."

I returned Beth's salute. "Very well, Sergeant, keep up the good work and I'll see you on the other side."

It was now time for the of two us to get to work. We both closed our eyes in preparation for our first transfer.

Within seconds my transfer was complete, I now found myself sitting on our front lawn chewing on a big fat juicy worm. YUCK! I quickly spit out what I could and immediately took to flight.

My destination was the hood of Tom's car. I wanted to see the whites of his eyes before we taught him a lesson he will never forget as long as he lives.

The second I landed on the hood of his car he turned and looked right at me. It scared me at first, until I reassured myself he wasn't looking at me, he was looking at a cute little robin who was about to make his day a whole lot worse.

"Beth, what's your status of repositioning the flock into the old oak tree?" I asked.

"General, the majority of the troops are already in position. All the troops and I will be ready to attack on your command."

"Well done, Sergeant!"

My job now was to get Tom out of his car. I realized I only had one round of ammunition in me and I needed to place that one round just outside the range of his windshield wipers if I wanted him to exit his car.

So I then flew directly toward his windshield as fast as I could fly. I was just about to slam into the glass when I changed course and flew straight up in the air. When I was about two feet above his windshield I released my payload.

I wasn't sure if I hit the mark, so I flew back around to see if I was successful. I couldn't have asked for a better placement! His wipers were now hard at work trying to erase my nasty secretion from his windshield. Too bad for Tom his wipers weren't an inch longer, because if they were, he wouldn't have had to get out of his car to clean up my mess.

"Beth, I have successfully left a nasty looking stain on Tom's windshield just out of the range of his wipers. It should only be a matter of seconds before he exits his car."

"Danny, all of our troops are now in position and we are now waiting for your command to attack."

"Good job, Sergeant! Or should I say Master Sergeant?"

"Master Sergeant does have a nice ring to it," said Beth.

When I looked inside Tom's car, I could see that he was now anxiously searching the interior of his glove compartment looking for something to clean off his windshield.

Then, just as I predicted, he exited his car in preparation to get rid of the mess that I had left him.

As soon as he closed his car door and leaned over his windshield to clean it, I gave the command to attack.

"Beth, commence bombing the target!"

At this point, both Beth and I were transferring into each individual robin at an unbelievable pace dropping numerous payloads on the target. When the dust finally cleared, the target had already retreated back into his car.

I looked down at the ground where he was standing. I was amazed to see there was hardly any bird poop on the ground. I then flew down to investigate. When I looked inside Tom's car I saw him sitting there covered with bird poop. I could tell by his actions that he was quite upset, to say the least. He was now having trouble even getting the key into his car's ignition.

It was then I asked Beth to look for reinforcements.

"Beth, are there any other birds in the area, other than those robins, that can help finish off Tom's car?"

"I see a few crows in the adjacent tree," said Beth. "I'll see if I can get them to help us finish off the target."

"It's too late, Beth," I screamed. "He's getting away."

Then out of nowhere I saw these three crows go whizzing by me on an intercept course with Tom's getaway car. Beth was able to score a few more hits on the fleeing vehicle before it raced out of sight.

Even though Beth and I don't wear superhero costumes and we don't have superhero names, today we have proven we are a force to be reckoned with. So, in the future, watch out all you criminals, because there are a couple of new sheriffs in town and their names are Danny and Beth Steiner.

Chapter Twelve

A Call for Help

It was about nine o'clock in the morning when Beth and I finally made our way downstairs for breakfast. Everything seemed to be normal. It wasn't until we entered our kitchen that we realized there was a problem.

Like clockwork our mother has never failed to set the table for breakfast in the past, but for some reason this morning that didn't happen. There were no plates, no spoons, not even a fork anywhere in sight.

After staring at the kitchen table for a short period of time, Beth and I turned and looked at each other. "What's going on?" asked Beth.

"I don't know. Let's just set the table, and then we'll both go check on Mom."

As soon as we were done setting the table, my mother came walking into the kitchen. Her destination was the cabinet in which we kept all our dishes. It was obvious to me that she was unaware of our presence. It wasn't until she started reaching into the cabinet to grab some plates that I decided to question her actions.

"Mom, what are you doing?"

She turned and looked at us. "Good morning, I didn't see you two standing there." She then looked over at the kitchen table. "Wow, I should be late for breakfast more often."

Worried about my mother's health, I asked her if she was Ok.

"Don't worry about me. I'm just not myself today," she replied.

Beth quickly spoke up. "Are you sick?"

"No, Beth! I'm not sick!"

"Then what's the problem?" I asked.

"There was this sad news story on TV this morning and it really struck a chord with me."

Never in my life have I ever seen my mother so affected by a single news story. "Mom, bad news is a daily occurrence in today's world. What makes today's news any different than any other day's news?"

"Danny, at seven fifteen this morning three escaped prisoners entered a preschool in Courtland, New York, and took thirty-one people hostage. Twenty-eight of them were preschool-aged children. These three felons are now threatening to do something bad to all thirty-one hostages if their demands are not met by three o'clock this afternoon."

So I said, "Wow! That really is a sad story. Now, I understand why you're upset."

Beth then asked, "Were there any animals taken hostage?"

"Beth, aren't thirty-one human lives enough?" My mother asked.

"I'm sorry Mom, I didn't mean anything by it."

"Come to find out," said my mom, "I do remember them saying there was a dog inside the school at the time of the takeover."

"What kind of dog was it?" Beth asked.

"I think it was a Saint Bernard," Mom replied.

"Danny, that's really good news!" Beth exclaimed.

"Beth, I think you need some professional help," said my mother.

Luckily for Beth, my mother's cell phone started ringing in the other room. As my mother ran out of the kitchen to answer her phone, I leaned over and whispered to Beth, "What are you doing? You're going to give away our secret."

"Danny, forget the stupid secret. There are thirty-one innocent peoples' lives in danger and we have the ability to save them. Danny, if we don't do something to help them, we will both regret it for the rest of our lives."

"Beth, you're not the one to tell Mom."

"If that is the case, then you tell her!"

Right then my mother came walking back into the kitchen "Tell her what?" my mother asked.

I quickly changed the subject. "Mom! Who was on the phone?"

"It was Ted. He wants the three of us to come down to the shelter right away!"

"It sounds important; did he tell you what it is about?" I asked.

"Danny!" shouted Beth. "You know what it is about! He's going to ask for our help to free the hostages!"

"Beth, what's wrong with you?!" my mother shouted.

So I answer, "There isn't anything wrong with Beth, she just wants to help the hostages. If you drive us down to the shelter, Ted will explain everything to you."

"I hope so, because I'm about ready to blow a fuse," said my mom.

We dropped Scruffy off at Grandpa Jack's house on our way to the Animal Shelter.

Chapter Thirteen

The Secret Comes Out

· ·

As soon as we arrived at the animal shelter, Beth and I ran as fast as we could from our mother's car all the way to Ted's office without stopping. Normally we wouldn't leave our mother alone in an unfamiliar parking lot to fend for herself, but our desire to speak with Ted first made it necessary.

The second we entered Ted's office, he looked up from what he was working on. "If it isn't my two favorite Super Heroes, what brings you two here on this lovely summer morning?"

"You just called our mother and asked her to drive us over here!" said Beth.

"Come to think of it, I did call your mother," said Ted. "Where is she anyway?"

"Danny and I decided to run ahead," Beth explained. "She'll be here shortly."

"Are you two aware of the hostage situation taking place in Courtland, New York, today?"

"Yes we are!" shouted Beth.

"We're also aware there was a Saint Bernard inside the preschool when this all started," I added.

"While we're waiting for your mother," said Ted, "I'll fill you two in on what's been going on. Earlier this morning, I received a phone call from a Special Agent named Matt Stark of the FBI telling me about the hostage situation in Courtland, NY. After he was done giving me all the details, he then pleaded with me to put your dying old grandfather on a military helicopter and fly him up to Courtland so he could help the FBI out with this hostage situation. I reminded him that your grandfather was retired, but he didn't want to hear that."

"What did you say after that?" I asked.

"I told him that I would have to get clearance from one of your grandfather's doctors before I could send him to Courtland."

"So what did his doctor say?" asked Beth.

"I don't know, because I didn't even bother asking him. I don't need any doctor to tell me something I already know. Your grandfather is no longer capable of going on these missions, the helicopter ride alone would most likely kill him. So that left me with only one option, to send you two in his place. Because of your age, I normally wouldn't even think about asking you two to take your grandfather's place, but because there are twenty-eight preschool-aged children's lives hanging in the balance, I realized I wouldn't be able to live with myself if I didn't at least ask."

"Yes!" shouted Beth. "I'm ready to go right now."

Suddenly, our mother came storming into Ted's office with a disgusted look on her face. "Why in the world would you two leave me in my car and go running into a building that I'm not familiar with? I'm pretty sure if I remember right, I raised you two better than that. What do you two dummies have to say for yourselves?"

Neither Beth nor I even bothered to answer our mother's question; instead we admitted to our ignorance and apologized for our actions.

The second my mother accepted our apology, I introduced her to Ted. "Mom, this is Ted, he's the fellow who runs the animal shelter for Grandpa Jack."

"It's nice to finally get to meet you, Ted," Mom said.

Ted stood up and reached out to shake my mother's hand "It's a pleasure to meet you too, Mrs. Steiner."

For some reason my mother just froze up. I quickly realized that she was being affected by Ted's immense size. She stood there for nearly thirty seconds without saying a word before she finally responded. "I'm sorry, Ted, for reacting this way, the kids never told me."

"Don't worry about it," said Ted. "This happens all the time. I've realized over the years, when you're as handsome as I am, a lot people are going to stop and stare at you." The room suddenly became very quiet, because the one adjective you'd never use to describe Ted's appearance would be the word handsome. So there we all stood in total silence, until Ted started laughing uncontrollably, at which time we all started laughing along with him.

Once we were done laughing, Ted asked us all to be seated.

My mother sat at one end of the desk, while Beth and I sat at the other.

"Before I get started I need to set up a couple of ground rules," said Ted. "Danny and Beth, I need you to remain silent the entire time I'm talking to your mother."

Realizing that it would be difficult for me and nearly impossible for Beth, I asked Ted if he had a roll of tape.

He reached into a drawer and pulled out a large roll of duct tape and handed it to me.

"Desperate times require desperate measures," I said.

I quickly ripped off two good size pieces of tape and placed one piece of tape on my mouth and handed Beth the other. She wasted no time placing the second piece over her own mouth.

"I don't know what's going on, but it must be very important if Danny and Beth are willing to tape their mouths closed without anyone asking them to do so."

"The word important is an understatement. I would describe this discussion that we're about to have as being life changing."

"If that is the case, then I'm all ears," said my Mom.

"Before we get started, did your late husband ever mention the word TRANSFERANCE?"

"That's funny you asked, because just before he died, he told me that someday someone was going to ask me that same question. He also told me to tell that person that whenever he attempted to do a transfer, he would get physically sick, whatever that means."

"Wow, you've just answered a question that a lot of people around here have been wondering about for the last twenty years," said Ted

"So what does the word transference have to do with anything?" asked my mother.

"To start with, the word transference can be found in any dictionary, but the meaning we use for that same word is totally different from the one you'll find in your dictionary."

"Why is that?" my mother asked.

"Because, the majority of the people on this planet wouldn't even believe what I'm about to tell you exists. So, to make a long story short, here is our meaning of the word transference. TRANSFERANCE is the Super Human ability for oneself to be able to transfer his or her inner being into another living creator."

"I'm sorry, Ted, I don't read comic books and I definitely don't believe in super human abilities like that one."

"Mrs. Steiner, what would you say if I told you that Danny and Beth both possess this power and on several occasions they've used it?"

"Ted, I don't know what kind of junk you're putting into my kids' heads, but you must stop it immediately."

"Mrs. Steiner, if what I'm telling isn't true, explain to me what happened at the zoo the other day."

My mother just sat there in shock. You could tell that she was trying somehow to make sense out of the whole situation. She then turned and looked over at me and Beth.

"Is it true you two were behind all those strange happenings that took place at the zoo the other day?"

Beth quickly ripped the tape off of her mouth. "Mom, that's only a small sample of what Danny and I can do. Ted thinks we're ready to go on our first mission."

"Hold everything," shouted my mother. "What mission!?"

Beth quickly reapplied the tape to her mouth realizing that things might get a little ugly.

"Mrs. Steiner, are you aware of the preschool hostage situation in Courtland, New York?"

"Yes, I'm very much aware of the twenty-eight children and three adults being held hostage in upstate New York."

"I'll get straight to the point. The FBI needs Beth and Danny's help to free the hostages."

"As much as I feel bad for those hostages, I am not willing to risk my own children's lives to save theirs."

"You wouldn't be risking your children's lives. Danny and Beth will be kept at a safe distance away from the preschool and protected by an armed FBI agent at a secure location."

"That is well and good, Ted, but what happens to them if they witness something really terrible? Can you promise me they won't see something that might affect them mentally for the rest of their lives?"

"I must admit," said Ted. "I can't guarantee that won't happen."

My mother then turned and looked directly at me and Beth.

"Danny and Beth take the tape off your mouths," said my mother.

Beth and I both removed the tape.

"Danny and Beth, do you understand the risk involved with this mission?" my mother asked.

"Yes, Mom, we understand the risks," said the two of us.

"I will let you two go under one condition: Danny will be the one who connects with the Saint Bernard, and Beth, you will only be there as backup."

"That's not fair," shouted Beth, "my powers are stronger than Danny's!"

"Beth, Danny is older than you are and less likely to be affected by what he sees. Beth, you have a choice, you can either come with us to New York or you can stay with Grandpa Jack and Steve until we return."

"I see your point now," said Beth. "I'll willing to play second fiddle if it gets me a ride to New York."

My mother then turned and looked at Ted. "I am willing to let Danny and Beth go to New York and help the FBI save the hostages under the following conditions. Condition number one, Danny, Beth and I remain together the entire time we are in New York. Condition number two, Danny will be used only as a spy. Last, but not least, Beth will only be used if Danny becomes ill or cannot perform his duties. Ted, do we have a deal?" asked my mother.

Ted agreed to my mother's demands, and they both shook hands to seal the agreement.

Ted then drove the four of us to a nearby army reserve base where a military helicopter was standing by to take us to Courtland, NY.

Chapter Fourteen

The Journey

. . . .

T he four of us were now on our way to Courtland, New York, onboard a US Army Blackhawk helicopter. Our first line of business when we arrived in Courtland was to meet up with an FBI Agent named Matt Stark.

We'd been flying for a little over an hour when one of the crew members came back to talk to us.

"Excuse me, the pilot has asked me to inform you that we will be landing in a matter of minutes. So please stay seated until the aircraft has come to a complete stop."

"Thank you, Sergeant!" said Ted.

"Sir, before I go, I just wanted to wish you good luck in saving those children's lives today."

"Sergeant, I'm just along for the ride. It's those two kids sitting right there who are going to pull this miracle off."

The sergeant then turned around and looked at the two of us. You could tell by the look on his face that he had his doubts.

Beth then reached out and grabbed the man's arm and pulled him in closer to her.

"That's a scary thought, isn't it, Sergeant?" said Beth.

Beth then started giggling, while the sergeant smiled at us and wished us both good luck.

They landed our helicopter at one of the local ball fields. As we were exiting the chopper, I noticed that there were a lot of people in the adjacent parking lot. You didn't have to be a rocket scientist to realize these were the family members of the thirty-one hostages being held at the preschool.

While we were being escorted through the parking lot by one of the local police officers, I heard several people asking the same question. "Who are these people?"

Beth wasn't going to let this moment go by without of one her trademark comments. "We are the Steiner kids and we're about to open a can of whoop ass on three unsuspecting kidnappers. So stop your crying, because we'll have your kids home in no time."

I don't think the crowd took Beth's comment seriously due to her age.

After that I started hearing several other individuals asking a different question: "Who are these Steiner kids?"

Beth would have answered that question too, if it wasn't for my mother's hand being placed over her mouth.

From the ball field, we were then driven to a checkpoint just up the street from where the Courtland Preschool was located.

The checkpoint was being manned by a couple of local police officers. Standing next to the officers was a gray-haired old man wearing an FBI jacket. You could tell he was waiting for us. You could also tell just by looking at him he wasn't having a good day. He made it a point to get right up into Ted's face as soon as Ted exited the car. I honestly thought there was going to be a fight.

Ted smiled at the FBI Agent. "Matt, long time no see, what have you been doing with yourself lately?"

That is when Agent Stark started yelling at Ted. "Let me guess, Jack was too sick to make the trip!?"

"He wanted to come, but his doctor wouldn't let him," said Ted.

Agent Stark continued yelling. "So let me get this straight, you wasted three and a half hours of my valuable time and a bunch of taxpayers' money to fly up here to tell me something you could have done in two minutes just by calling me on my cell phone!"

"Matt, I've got five words to say to you."

"Ted, I'll give you seven words! People might die because of your actions!"

"I think you will like my five words better! Say hello to Jack's grandkids."

It was amazing how quickly Agent Stark's demeanor changed with this new reality. "Ted, don't just stand there, introduce me to these two fine young people!"

Ted then brought Special Agent Stark over to where I was standing.

"This is Danny Steiner. He's presently the team leader. Danny, like his sister, has the ability to make transfers without the use of the chamber."

"I didn't know that was possible," said Agent Stark as he shook my hand.

"It is now!" said Ted. "That's not all. What makes these two even more special is they have the ability to work as a team even in the most difficult situations."

"Impressive!" said Agent Stark:

Now it was Beth's turn to be introduced to Agent Stark.

Beth quickly spoke up. "Don't waste your breath, Ted! It's nice to meet you, Special Agent Stark." As she stood there with this big smile on her face shaking Agent Stark's hand, she added, "My name is Beth! Don't let this pretty exterior fool you, I'm just as smart as Danny and my powers are even more developed than his. This is why I believe I should be the one making the connection with the dog inside the preschool during today's mission."

Agent Stark turned and looked over at Ted for some input.

"Matt, due to the sensitive nature of this situation and Beth's young age, Mrs. Steiner, Beth's mother, has asked that we only use her daughter as backup in case Danny is unable to perform his duties."

Agent Stark first looked over at my mother and then looked back at Beth. "Beth, I have to agree with your mother. Hostage situations can get quite messy. You're better off being on the sidelines for now."

"At least I'm still Danny's backup," said Beth. "Good luck, big brother, I hope you break a leg!"

She followed that up with some of her insane laughter.

Beth's off the mark comment really struck a chord with me. It wasn't until that moment in time that I realized I was way over my head when it came to this rescue mission. What was I thinking when I volunteered to come here? This is when I wished my mother would change her mind and let Beth get involved.

Special Agent Stark then walked over to meet my mother.

"It's a pleasure to meet you Mrs. Steiner. I want to thank you for allowing your son and daughter to come here today to help us free the hostages."

"I just hope they'll make a difference," said my mother.

"I'm one hundred percent sure that lives will be saved today with the help of your children."

My mother then smiled at Agent Stark.

"Ted, you know the routine, so there is no need for me to stick around and complicate the situation." Agent Stark then pointed at a small group of FBI agents standing behind a barricade just a short distance down the road. "I'll be standing right over there. So as soon as you and Danny have figured out the locations of the three escaped prisoners and the thirty-one hostages, contact me immediately."

Agent Stark then reached out and shook my hand one last time. "Good luck, kid, there are a lot of people counting on you."

I was so scared; I couldn't even respond to his statement.

Beth somehow sensed my fear and reached out and grabbed my arm. "Don't worry, big brother, I've got your back!"

I knew right then and there that Beth was planning on joining me inside the preschool. What I couldn't figure out was how she would pull this off with my mother watching her like a hawk, but I knew in the end she was somehow going to be there.

Chapter Fifteen

The Making of a Superhero

After our meeting with Special Agent Matt Stark, Ted escorted the three of us over to what I can only describe as an armored van. The entire outside of this strange-looking van was covered with thick steel plates, not a window in sight.

Standing guard outside of that same van was a young FBI Agent with a forty-five caliber pistol strapped to his side.

As soon as Beth got close, she decided to take this opportunity to greet the young man. "Hi there! How's it going? Killed anybody lately?"

"Young lady, please stand back!" said the agent. "This is a top secret van and only authorized FBI agents are allowed inside."

"Impressive!" replied Beth.

Ted quickly stepped forward and whipped out his FBI badge and photo ID and showed it to the agent. I almost fell over when I saw it. This whole time Ted was an FBI agent and he never told us.

As soon as the young agent had completed verifying Ted's credentials, he walked over to the van door and held it open so the four of us could enter.

Beth was just about to enter the van when she stopped, turned and looked up at the young agent. "You've got to ask yourself, why in the world would the FBI invite two punk kids into a highly classified area during a hostage situation?" She then added, "It boggles the mind when you think about."

The agent just stood there with this puzzled look on his face. Beth had left the young man speechless, like so many others before him.

Once inside the van, I noticed there were various types of communication and surveillance equipment scattered throughout the high tech vehicle. However, there was one piece of equipment that stood out more than all the rest. There sitting smack dab in the middle of the van floor was another one of my grandfather's famous transference chambers. It was an older version, but according to Ted it still worked.

After a brief tour of the interior of the van we all sat down. Beth and my mother chose to get comfortable on a couch that was facing several TV monitors, each one of the monitors showing a different camera angle of the preschool, including the various law enforcement agents who were currently surrounding it.

Ted and I sat at a small table near the rear of the van. On the table in front of us rested a manila folder with the word TOP SECRET stamped all over it.

Inside that folder there were several documents such as the rap sheets on each individual kidnapper, the names and ages of the thirty-one hostages, and several drawings showing the interior of the preschool as well as its floor plan. On the very bottom of the pile of documents lay a small white envelope with the name "Thor" written on it. "Ted, I wonder what is in this envelope."

"It's most likely a picture of the Saint Bernard you'll be using for your host animal during today's mission. Go ahead and open it."

When I opened it, I discovered Ted was right, inside the envelope was a picture of a full grown Saint Bernard surrounded by a bunch of preschool-age kids with big smiles on their faces. On the back of the picture, someone had written, "Thor's first day as the school's new mascot."

"Ted, it turns out the dog is the school's mascot."

"Danny, that's just one more reason why you have to keep that dog out of harm's way."

Once we were finished reviewing all of the documents, it was time for me to get to work. To start with, I moved to a more comfortable chair hoping it would make things a little easier on myself. I then closed my eyes and within a couple of seconds I found myself not on the inside of the preschool as I'd planned, but on the outside trying to look in.

I quickly checked out my surroundings. Standing just to the right of me was a police officer holding a leash that was attached to a collar that adorned my neck.

It was obvious that I'd missed my target and I was now a police dog awaiting my next command from my handler.

So I closed my eyes for a second time. This time I pictured Thor's photograph in my head. When I finally opened my eyes this time, I was taken aback by what I saw. I now understood why there was so much fuss about keeping Beth on the sidelines. Seeing young children being abused is a very painful experience.

All I wanted to do now was to find those three sick individuals who had done this and tear them apart with my mighty canines, but first I had to check in with Ted.

"Ted! I've got good news and bad news. Which one do you want first?"

"Give me the good news first!" said Ted.

"I completed my transfer and I'm in full control of one very large adult Saint Bernard named Thor, and I'm ready to get to work."

I could hear my mother and Beth cheering in the background over my success.

"Good job, Danny!" said Ted. "Now what's the bad news?"

"The kidnappers have tied up and gagged every one of these poor little kids. To make things worse, they've even lined them up against one of the exterior walls of the preschool so they can be used as human shields. I'm so mad, I'm about ready to make chew toys out of all three of these kidnappers!"

"Danny, listen to me! We sent you in to that preschool for one reason only, to spy on the kidnappers. If you think biting one of these three armed individuals is a good idea, you're gravely mistaken. You run the risk of getting innocent people killed as well as the dog you are presently attached to. So do me a favor and leave that part of the job to the FBI. They'll take care of those creeps for you. Danny, do you understand what I'm saying to you?"

"Yes, Ted, I'm a spy and only a spy, so stick to the plan."

"Good! Now the first thing I need for you to do is to verify the location, and the physical condition of all the hostages."

"Ok Ted." So I did exactly what Ted asked me to do.

About five minutes later I contacted Ted again. "Ted, I counted up these children, not once, but several times. Each time I've counted them, I've come up with the same number, twenty-nine kids. Somehow the authorities got the number of kids wrong when they said there were twenty-eight of them."

"Danny, I would rather have one extra child than one less. Now tell me exactly where are they located and what their physical condition is."

"All twenty-nine kids are lined up against the rear exterior wall of the playroom. As far as I can tell, they all look to be in good health."

"Good! Now what's the status of the three teachers?"

"Just like the children, they have been tied up, gagged and are also being held hostage inside the playroom, but unlike the children they're located on the opposite wall just to the right of, door that leads into the bathroom. All three teachers seem to be in good health. There is only one small discrepancy, one of the teachers has a fat lip and a small bloodstain on her blouse."

"Danny, what do we know about the bad guys?"

"I can only see one of the kidnappers. Based on the photographs I saw in that FBI folder, it's definitely Frank Glitch, the oldest, the meanest and most likely the leader of the pack. He's presently sitting in a chair next to the door that leads into the front office and he's holding a shotgun on his lap. I won't lie to you; this guy really creeps me out."

"Danny, do you have any idea where the other two kidnappers are located?"

"According to my superhuman hearing, aka my standard dog ears, they are both located inside the main office in the front of the building. I know this, because I can hear two distinct male voices coming from the other side of the door."

"Danny, that's good to know, but I need their exact location inside of the front office and what kind of weapons they have in their possession."

"Since dogs don't have thumbs, how do you expect me to open this door so I can gain access into the front office?"

"It's really simple, just go over to the door and start barking your fool head off until someone opens the door for you."

"Ted, do I have to remind you that Frank Glitch is guarding that door and he still has that really big shotgun in his possession?"

"Danny, don't let him scare you. The worst thing that could happen is he shoots you, at which time you'll automatically return back to your human body."

"Ted, if he shoots me, will it hurt?"

"Danny, it will only hurt for a few of seconds until you've completed your transfer back into your own body. The worst part of being shot is the memory you're going to have for the rest of your life of being a witness to your own murder."

"Thanks, Ted! I really feel safe now! Next time could you do me a favor and just lie to me?"

"Danny, he won't risk shooting you because he knows the FBI will rush the building the second they hear shots fired. So just do what I tell you."

"Ok, here goes nothing."

So I walked over to the door leading into the front office and started barking my fool head off. The next thing I knew I had a shotgun pointed right at my head, but I'm just a stupid dog and I don't know anything about shotguns, so I just continued barking. Luckily for me one of the kidnappers from inside the front office opened the door and most likely saved my life.

"What's going on in here?" asked this second kidnapper.

"This stupid dog won't shut up. I think he wants me to blow his fool head off. So take him in there with you two before I silence him forever."

The second kidnapper looked down at me and said, "You'll be safer in here with us. Uncle Carl and Uncle Pete will take good care of you."

So I quickly made my way into the front office and found a safe place to lie down. From where I was lying I could see the entire office.

"Ted, I'm in the front office."

"Danny, what do you see?"

"Pete, aka the Freak, is sitting at the desk playing with a very large knife. He also has what looks like a Colt pistol resting on the desk next to where he is sitting. Carl, aka the Butcher, is lying down on the floor and peeking out of a curtain that covers the large picture window just to the right of the front entrance. He's got a rifle with a scope on it."

"Good work, Danny, I'm going to leave the van for a short period of time so I can brief Agent Stark. I'll be back shortly."

I then heard the FBI van door open and close.

Ted hadn't been gone five minutes when Carl the Butcher and Pete the Freak started plotting how they were going to go into the playroom and take Frank's shotgun away from him. I thought it was just talk until Pete stood up and tucked his knife into his pants and told Carl that he was going to go to the bathroom now. The plan was Pete would go to the bathroom and on his way back from the bathroom he was going to use his knife to get the drop on Frank. Once he had Frank subdued, Pete would then call out Carl's name at which time Carl was to come into the playroom and take possession of Frank's shotgun.

Pete then walked over to the door that led to the playroom, opened it, entered the playroom and closed the door behind him.

I had no clue on how to stop this chain of events that was already in progress, so out of pure desperation, I disconnected from Thor, the Saint Bernard, and ran over to where my mother and Beth were sitting. With tears in my eyes, I stood there and begged my mother to go get Ted.

Without hesitation, my mother got up off the couch and ran out the door to get Ted.

Beth grabbed my arm. "Get ahold of yourself, Danny! Now briefly tell me what's going on."

So I told her that the two kidnappers in the front office were about to overthrow the third kidnapper, their leader.

She grabbed my hand and dragged me back to my seat and told me to sit down. Then she walked over to the van door and locked it so no one could enter.

"What are you doing, Beth?" I asked.

"I'm taking over!" she said. "Now hurry up and reconnect with the Saint Bernard and start barking your fool head off again."

"What will that do?" I asked.

"I'm hoping it will make the kidnappers nervous so they postpone their mutiny."

"That's not a bad idea!" So without hesitation, I reconnected with the Saint Bernard and started barking my fool head off for the second time. Within a few of seconds Frank came charging into the front office pointing his shotgun at my head threatening to blow it off. Luckily for me, Pete was returning from the bathroom at almost the same time. Frank heard Pete coming and spun around and pointed the shotgun at him.

"I don't know why this stupid dog is barking again, but one of you two better get him to stop it right now or I'm going to shoot both of you!" said Frank. He then returned to the playroom and slammed the door behind him.

"Good news, Beth, Pete was unable to get the drop on Frank and everything is back the way it was before the attempted overthrow. So you can unlock the door now."

"It's too late for that" said Beth! "I have an idea on how you and I can take out these three escaped convicts without any outside help."

What I'd feared all these years had finally come true. Beth has gone bonkers and I just happen to be locked up in the same van with her. Lucky me!"

Chapter Sixteen

Beth Unleashed

. . . .

My little sister, Beth, has somehow convinced herself that if we work together we can defeat the three armed kidnappers who are presently holding thirty-two people hostage.

If you ask me, I think she's lost a few of her marbles.

Knowing that my mother and Ted would soon be returning to the FBI van, I decided the best course of action would be for me to unlock the van door prior to their arrival. So I disconnected from the school's mascot named Thor, stood up and started walking towards the van door.

Suddenly Beth caught up to me from behind and somehow managed to drag me down to the floor. I was amazed at how strong she was. Her desire to maintain control of this situation had somehow made her stronger than I remembered.

"Danny, stop what you're doing and listen to what I have to say to you!" yelled Beth.

"Beth, I don't want to hurt you, so please let go of me."

"Danny, give me a chance to explain my reasoning. If you're still not convinced by the time I'm done talking, I will unlock the door myself and I will do it without any further discussion."

The terms of Beth's agreement were too good to pass up. So without hesitation, I agreed to listen to whatever she had to say.

"Danny, do you know what today is?" asked Beth.

"Let me see, I'm pretty sure it's Wednesday."

"Today is the day you and I join the ranks of all those other Super Heroes that came before us."

"What other Super Heroes?" I asked. "The only Super Heroes I'm even aware of are the ones they write about in comic books.

As much as I would like for them to exist in the real world, they only exist in the minds of their readers."

"Ok, try this one on for size," said Beth. "Do you remember what Grandpa Jack said about me? He told you that someday in the near future, I would amaze you beyond belief. Danny, today is that day!"

"I'm still not convinced, Beth. You've got to do better than that if you think you're going to change my mind."

"Ok Danny, you've left me no other option. Prepare to have your mind blown. While you and Thor were scoping out the interior of the preschool, I was sitting on the couch with my eyes closed searching the local woods for a host animal that might possess the special qualifications that we would need to overthrow these three villains. Luckily for us, I found the perfect candidate. You'll never in a million years guess what type of creature I ended up connecting with."

You don't have to be a genius to know that there aren't any animals on the entire North American continent that could possibly possess the qualifications that Beth was referring to. I wasn't sure what Beth was up to, but I was guessing she was trying to buy some time. For what? I had no clue, but I was willing to play along with her silly little game by guessing a mythical creature that only exists in fairy tales and tall stories. "Beth, I'm guessing you connected with a unicorn!"

"Danny, don't be silly, everyone knows there is no such animal as the unicorn! The creature I actually connected with was a full grown adult Bigfoot!"

I probably would have fallen over laughing if I wasn't already on the floor. "Beth, Bigfoots don't exist! So do me a favor, stop talking and go unlock the door like you promised."

"Danny, answer me this question. Would a full-grown adult Bigfoot have the qualifications we would need to take out these three escaped prisoners?"

"If a Bigfoot actually did exist, a full-grown adult Bigfoot would probably be the most perfect animal on this entire planet to pull off such a miracle," I acknowledged.

"Danny, I want to ask you one last question before I get up and unlock the door," said Beth. "Is there anything I can do to prove to you that I have a Bigfoot waiting out in the woods ready to help us?"

I had to think for a minute before it came to me. "Yes there is! According to legend, Bigfoots are capable of communicating with each over very long distances by using a series of loud hoots and hollers. Let's see if you can get your imaginary Bigfoot to scream really loud for me."

"Ok!" said Beth.

While Beth lay on the floor with her eyes closed, I quietly stood up and started heading towards the van door in preparation to unlock it. Suddenly, I heard this mighty "RRROOOAAARR!" that came from far out in the woods. Never in my life had I heard anything remotely like it. You could tell by the extreme volume of the roar that it came from a very large creature.

I turned around and looked Beth straight in the eye. "I must admit, that was pretty good, but I'm still not convinced. How do I know that wasn't a full grown black bear making that loud noise?"

Beth shook her head in disgust. "Danny, they say a picture is worth a thousand words. If that is the case, why don't close your eyes and check out my imaginary Bigfoot for yourself?"

So that is exactly what I did. Within about thirty of seconds, I had completed my transfer. Beth's description of her imaginary Bigfoot did not prepare me for what I was about to experience. When I finally opened my eyes I was taken aback by the sheer, size of the creature. He stood nearly eight-foot-tall and weighed in excess of three hundred pounds. He had arms and legs the size of tree trunks and he smelled like he hadn't taken a bath in a very long time. I was just about to take this Bigfoot out for a test drive when suddenly I lost my connection. The next thing I knew I found myself back at the van lying spread eagled on the floor. With my eyes still closed, I could hear Beth laughing her fool head off.

I sat up, opened my eyes and looked over at Beth. "Beth, what just happened to me?"

"Danny, shortly after you made your transfer, your body went limp and you fell to the floor."

"I don't understand what just happened, we both have made numerous transfers before while we were in a standing position and neither one of us has ever fallen down before."

"That's not true. Do you remember the other day when we were at the zoo and I had that goat chase you across the entire length of that animal enclosure?"

"Yes, I remember."

"You thought I called off the attack when you screamed for help. You were wrong. I didn't call off the attack; instead, like you, I lost my connection and found myself lying on the ground. If you and Mom had only turned around a little sooner, you both would have seen me lying on the ground."

"It must have something to do with the distance between where our human bodies are located in comparison to our where host bodies are situated. So from now on, I'll remember either be sitting down or lying down before I make any long distance transfers."

"Danny, did you connect with my imaginary Bigfoot?"

"Beth, you were right and I was wrong. You are smart and I am dumb. Are you happy now?"

"I accept your apology. What did you think about my Bigfoot?" asked Beth.

"Beth, your Bigfoot is awesome! The only problem is he smells really, really bad. I don't think he's ever taken a bath in his entire life."

All of a sudden, the knob on the van door started turning. I froze like a deer caught in the headlights of an oncoming car.

"Danny and Beth, unlock this door right now!" screamed our mother.

Besides Mom's voice, I could hear Ted talking in the background.

Beth quickly realized that our mother's screaming had freaked me out. I couldn't help it. All these years I've been the good son, while Beth played the role of the monster.

"It's now or never, Danny!" said Beth. "Either you're a Super Hero or you're not! You make the call!"

I thought to myself, a true Super Hero lives his or her life on the edge. It's now time for me to stop fearing the unknown and step outside of the box and discover who the real Danny Steiner is.

"Mom!" I shouted. "Beth and I have decided to do this entire mission on our own!"

I could hear Mom and Ted talking, but I couldn't make out exactly what they were saying.

"Ted!" I shouted. "Please do me a big favor and tell Special Agent Stark to make sure that no one shoots the Bigfoot!"

Beth started clapping over my response. "Danny, you won't regret your decision, together you and I will make history!"

"Bigfoot?" screamed my Mom. "What the hell is he talking about?"

"Mrs. Steiner, let me talk to your kids for you," said Ted.

"Danny, your grandfather connected with a Bigfoot several years ago. You've chosen a magnificent creature, good luck with your first mission. I will see you and Beth when it's all over."

"Ted, I'm not the one controlling the Bigfoot, Beth is!"

"So you two have teamed up. This is exactly what your grandfather had predicted. I wish he was here right now so he could see you two in action."

Beth then got up off the floor and yelled out, "Ted, tell Special Agent Stark I plan on taking my Bigfoot right through the front door in about twenty minutes, so plan accordingly!"

"Good luck, Danny and Beth!" yelled Ted.

"Mrs. Steiner, let's go back to the preschool so we can get a front row seat for this main event."

"Have all three of you gone crazy?" asked my mother from the other side of the door. "Beth is too young to be involved in such a dangerous mission."

"Mrs. Steiner, you're wrong about that. Beth's level of maturity is far greater than the years she has spent on this earth."

Somehow, Ted was able to get our mother to leave with him. How he did it will always be a mystery to me.

"Danny, let's get to work," said Beth. "We need to sit next to each other during the entire operation, so we have good communications. I will be counting on you and Thor to tell me what's going on inside the school."

After sitting down, we both closed our eyes in preparation to transfer to our prospective host animals. Within a blink of an eye

I was back in control of Thor and patiently waiting for Beth's arrival.

Chapter Seventeen

Beth Takes on the Kidnappers

I've reconnected with the Saint Bernard named Thor and I've been waiting patiently inside the preschool for almost half an hour for Beth and her Bigfoot to arrive.

Ten more minutes have passed and still no sign of Beth or her oversized primate.

"Beth, what's taking you so long?" I asked.

"Danny, when you're as big a target as I am, you realize it's a good idea to walk slowly so you don't ruffle anyone's feathers. I wish you were out here with me so you could see all these various law enforcement agents staring at me. If I had to guess, I would say they are at least two hundred strong and of those two hundred strong at least half have their guns pointing at me right this second. Boy! I hope Ted got the word out not to shoot the Bigfoot."

"Beth, I'm sure he did, now answer this question for me. What do you plan on doing when you finally arrive at the school?"

"Let me see, first I plan on knocking down the front door. Once inside, I plan on opening a can of whoop ass and beating the crap out of each and every one of those three escaped convicts. I think that pretty much sums it up."

"That would be a great idea, Beth, if nobody had any guns, but since all three of these felons are carrying, there's an excellent chance that you and your Bigfoot will be shot shortly after you enter the building."

"Danny, what do you suggest?"

"Prior to your attack, you've got to first let the kidnappers observe your Bigfoot from a distance. Once they have seen he's as big as a full grown grizzly bear and twice as scary, the fear of death will then be planted into their brains. The anxiety that comes with the possibility of dying will cause them to freak out. The irrational thinking that follows should help give you and your Bigfoot the advantage to overthrow these three creeps."

"How am I supposed to do all of that?" Beth asked.

"I will help you. First, I want you to position your Bigfoot in front of the preschool so he can easily be seen from any of the school's front windows. When you're in position, Thor and I will get all three of these knuckleheads to look out the window at the same time. Then on my signal, I want you to roar as loud as you can for as long as you can."

"Danny, I'm just about at the front door now. They should have no problem seeing me from where I'm standing."

"Good, stay exactly where you are and wait for my signal."

"OK, Danny!" said Beth.

Both Pete the Freak and Carl the Butcher were sitting at the desk quietly eating some sandwiches that they had stolen from some of the kids' lunchboxes that they had found stored in the front office.

It was now time for me and Thor to go to work. I quickly positioned Thor just to the left of the front door and then together we started barking really loudly in the direction of the front door.

In a flash, both Carl the Butcher and Pete the Freak were standing at the picture window with their guns drawn peeking out from between the closed curtains trying to see what I was barking at.

"Wow! That is one really large Bigfoot," said Carl.

"I wonder where the FBI found him," said Pete. "I hope the heck he isn't planning on coming in here! I've heard that a full-grown Bigfoot can shatter a man's skull with one single blow to the head!"

"That's nothing!" said Carl. "I heard they eat your brains, too!"

"Bigfoots don't eat brains, stupid, it's the zombies that eat your brains!"

"Either way, Pete. We're both going to die!"

With Pete and Carl already showing signs of freaking out, it was now time to get Frank to come out and join the party. So I moved Thor closer to the playroom door and then we started barking loudly again.

Suddenly, Frank came barging into the front office with his shotgun in hand. "I warned you two idiots to keep that damn dog quiet, now I'm going to have to shoot both of you."

"Frank, before you waste any of your ammo on us, you better come check this out!" said Carl.

Frank walked over to the window and without any fear of being shot pulled the curtains wide open. "Wow! Halloween came early this year. That is one ugly Bigfoot costume," said Frank.

"That isn't a costume!" said Carl. "That is a real live Bigfoot standing right there!

"You're crazy!" said Frank.

"Beth, go ahead and roar really loud!" I said.

"Here goes nothing!" said Beth. "RRRRRROOOOOAAAAAARRRRRRR!!!"

Beth's roar was so loud it even scared the crap out of me and I knew it was coming. I expected the window panes to rattle, but I wasn't expecting to feel the vibration of Beth's roar coming through the floorboards below Thor's feet. Both Carl and Pete jumped at the same time when they heard Beth's mighty roar, but for some reason Frank didn't even flinch.

"Frank, what do you say now?" asked Pete.

"I say you two dummies don't have a brain between you. It's obvious the FBI is trying to scare us by using loudspeakers and amplifiers. I can take that costume wearing goofball out with just one bullet. He doesn't scare me one bit. I want you two to keep an eye on him and if he tries anything funny, shoot him for me!"

"OK!" said Pete.

Frank then pulled the curtains closed, returned to the playroom and slammed the door behind him.

"Beth, hurry up and find a place to hide before Pete and Carl look out the window again."

"When we're both dead," said Pete, "then Frank will know we were right."

"Pete, you stand guard at the door and I'll stay here and continue looking out this picture window," said Carl.

"Ok!" said Pete. Pete then walked over to the front door and pulled back the small curtain that covered the tiny window that was part of the front door.

"Carl, do you know what's worse than seeing a full-grown Bigfoot standing outside your front window?" asked Pete.

"What's that?" asked Carl.

"Having him disappear on you and not knowing what he's up to."

Carl quickly pressed his face tightly against the large picture window trying to see every square inch of that front yard. "I don't like it, Pete! He was just standing there a second ago! Where could he have gone?" asked Carl.

"Beth, where are you hiding right now," I asked.

"Danny, I'm standing on the side of the school building peeking around the corner," said Beth. "From here, I can see someone moving the bottom portion of the curtain the covers that large picture window."

"That's Carl. He's sitting on the floor peeking out window trying to locate you."

"Danny, I need you and Thor to get as far away from that picture window as possible, because I'm about to throw a really big rock right through that window."

I wasted no time moving Thor to the far corner of the room in preparation for Beth breaking the window.

Suddenly, this very large boulder came crashing through the picture window nearly taking Carl's head off in the process. Beth had thrown the giant rock so hard that it didn't hit the floor until after it bounced off the back wall of the front office.

Both Pete and Carl spun around to see the massive stone just lying there in the middle of the room surrounded by broken glass.

Suddenly, Beth reached in through the broken picture window with one of her gigantic Bigfoot hands and snatched Carl up by the nape of his neck. She then pulled him through what was left of the picture window cutting him in the process. It was quite impressive and scary at the same time. You could hear poor Carl crying for help the entire time Beth was dragging him away. I almost felt sorry for the creep.

"Quite impressive, Beth, remind me later never to mess with you again. Now what are you planning on doing with Carl?" I asked.

"I'm delivering him to a couple FBI agents standing out here next to a van."

I was just about to ask Beth a question when Frank came barging into the front office demanding to know what was going on.

Pete turned and looked at Frank with tears running down his face and said, "That Bigfoot just dragged Carl away like he was a bag of trash! Frank, he never had a chance to defend himself! I think we should give up and beg for mercy while we're still alive!"

"Are you crazy!?" screamed Frank. "I'll shoot you myself if you even attempt to give yourself up!"

Frank then turned and looked over in the direction of where Carl had been sitting. Carl's rifle was laying on the floor surrounded by shards of glass and some of Carl's blood.

"Two can play at this game!" yelled Frank. "I'll show them who is boss! Pete, keep an eye out for that overgrown ape! I'll be right back!" said Frank. He then retreated back to the playroom and slammed the door behind him for the second time.

"Danny!" said Beth. "Where is that other fellow who was in the front office with Carl?"

"His name is Pete and he's standing right behind the front door. He's waiting for you to return so he can shoot you."

"Danny, do me a favor and get Pete's attention away from the door temporarily so I can get a running start."

"Ok, Beth, give me five seconds and then start running!"

I knew barking wasn't going to work this time, so I had Thor latch on to one of Pete's pants legs and tug away. Still standing behind the door, Pete turned around and started smacking Thor on the top of his oversized canine head.

"Leave me alone you crazy mutt before I shoot you!" screamed Pete.

I continued to have Thor tug away on Pete's pants until I got Beth's final warning.

"Danny, get away from the front door right now!" shouted Beth.

"Not a problem!" I responded.

Without hesitation, I moved Thor away from the front door.

Too bad for Pete he didn't come with us.

In a blink of an eye, that solid wooden door came crashing right down right on top of old Pete knocking him out in the process. Using one of her massive Bigfoot hands, Beth reached down and grabbed hold of that heavy wooden door and hurled it across the room like it was a toy. She then reached down with her other gigantic Bigfoot hand and plucked Pete's unconscious body up from off the floor and flung him over her shoulder as she carried him away.

"Beth, hurry up back!" I cried out. "Frank is still in here with me and he is a lot meaner and he's ten times more dangerous that the first two clowns you just dragged out of here."

"Don't worry, big brother, I won't let the bad man hurt you!"

Suddenly, Frank came charging back into the front office. This time, he was dragging one of the adult female hostages by her hair and threatening to blow her head off with his shotgun if she didn't keep up with him. Once inside the room, he paused for a moment so he could assess the damages. "Damn! It looks like a bomb went off in here." He then turned and looked at me and Thor and said, "I'm amazed you're still alive. If I didn't know better, I would think that you and that monster of an ape were partners or something."

If he only knew! I thought to myself.

"Beth, be careful when you come back here, Frank has a hostage with him."

"Is it one of the little kids?" asked Beth.

"No, it's one of teachers. He's got a shotgun pointed at her head."

"Danny, I'll have to free that hostage first before I can save you."

"Just make it fast, so Thor and I don't get shot."

Frank and his hostage had now made their way across the room and were getting very close to where the front door of the preschool used to hang. He was no longer pulling her by her hair, but instead had his fingers wrapped around her skinny little neck and was choking her as he pushed her toward the front entrance. I had a feeling that Beth was now hiding just outside the front entrance, staying close to the exterior wall of the preschool so she couldn't be seen from inside the building. I think Frank knew this too, because he took his time carefully moving his hostage slowly out through the front entranc,e at the same time giving her plenty of opportunity to see what was just around the corner. Once outside, Frank's hostage caught sight of Beth's gigantic Bigfoot and screamed so loudly I think she woke up the dead.

Frank quickly pulled his hostage back inside the school building and threw her onto the floor. He then stood there with his shotgun pointing at the doorway waiting for Beth and her Bigfoot to come around the corner so he could shoot them.

I couldn't let Frank shoot my little sister and her Bigfoot, so I had Thor jump onto Frank's back and start biting at him.

Frank spun around, and Thor and I fell to the floor. Thor and I were just about to get back up when Frank fired a round of buckshot hitting us in our left hindquarter causing us immense pain. We were now out of commission and unable physically to help Beth any more.

When Franked turned back around after shooting me and Thor, Beth and her Bigfoot were standing just inside the doorway waiting to punish Frank for shooting us. Using the Bigfoot's massive hands, she grabbed the shotgun out of Frank's hands and then snapped it in two before throwing it across the room. Then using her gigantic Bigfoot fist, she punched Frank right in the face so hard he hit the back wall of the office and fell to the floor. He appeared to be unconscious.

Beth and her Bigfoot then carried the preschool teacher to safety, leaving Thor and me to suffer with our wounds.

"Danny, I'll be right back to help you and Thor."

I was in so much pain, I didn't realize Frank had somehow gotten back up on his feet and was now standing just inside the doorway holding Pete's revolver in his hand. It wasn't until Beth came back with her Bigfoot that I got a glimpse of Frank pointing the revolver right at Beth's Bigfoot's face.

"You messed with the wrong guy!" shouted Frank. "I'm going to send you to hell where you belong, you overgrown ape."

Suddenly, due to the extreme pain from Thor's wound, I lost my connection and found myself back inside the FBI van sitting in the chair where I had begun this operation.

I then heard a gunshot come from somewhere in the vicinity of the preschool building.

I ran over to check on Beth's human body, but there were no signs of life. All I could think was she died inside the Bigfoot and was unable to make it back to her body. I stood over her lifeless body and started crying.

Next thing I knew Beth sat up in the chair and started laughing at me. "Super Heroes don't cry!"

As I wiped the tears from my eyes, I asked Beth what happened to her and the Bigfoot after Thor and I passed out and I lost my connection.

"Luckily for me and the Bigfoot, the FBI grabbed Frank from behind causing him to shoot high, totally missing our head."

"Beth, we should go down to the school and see what's going on. I want to check on Thor and see if he's doing all right."

"Ok, let's go," said Beth.

Together, Beth and I ran all the way down to where Ted and our mother were standing. When we got there, we saw the Bigfoot carrying Thor's nearly lifeless body out of the school. The Bigfoot then placed Thor on the ground in front of some paramedics who were standing nearby.

The paramedics quickly went to work on Thor trying to save his live.

Our mother must have thought Beth and I were still connected to our host animals, because she started yelling at Bigfoot.

"Beth! You let your brother get shot. Your number one job was to protect your brother. If he dies, I will never forgive you."

Beth and I couldn't help but laugh.

My mother turned and looked at us when she heard us laughing.

"Just because you two are alive and unharmed doesn't mean you're out of the doghouse," said my mom.

Beth and I stood there with smiles on our faces knowing that everything was ok now, because of our actions.

Thor survived his wounds that day and returned to his job as school mascot. The Bigfoot returned to the woods and was never seen again. All hostages got home safely that night just as Beth had predicted. Last but not least, Ted treated the entire Steiner clan to a lovely dinner at a high-end restaurant.

Chapter Eighteen

Strangers Bearing Gifts

I t's been about a week since Beth and I helped capture those three escaped prisoners, in turn saving the lives of their thirty-two hostages. Since then, there have been no TV interviews, no award ceremonies, they never even bothered mentioning our names during any of the news broadcasts.

The only reason why I bring this up is because my mother is presently having a meeting with a couple of government officials in our kitchen. Beth and I both wanted to meet these two government representatives, but Mom sent us upstairs just prior to their arrival.

Beth, Scruffy and I were now waiting patiently up in my bedroom hoping for an invitation to join this conversation that was already in progress.

Suddenly, my cell phone started ringing. I was just about to answer it went Beth grabbed it out of my hands.

"Steiner residence!" said Beth. "What's your beef?"

Just by watching my sister's facial expressions, I knew she was talking to my mother.

I immediately jumped up and ran as fast as I could toward my bedroom door. Amazingly, I got there before Beth, but my lead soon diminished as we ran down the stairs. She passed me in the living room and crushed me by the time we got close to the kitchen. I swear my little sister is part jackrabbit.

Suddenly, Beth came to a screeching halt just outside the doorway that leads into our kitchen. I had all I could do to stop myself from running into her. As soon as I came to a complete stop, I looked inside our kitchen and saw my mother sitting at our kitchen table with a couple of gentlemen. The older of the two was wearing a Navy uniform, while the younger one was dressed in civilian attire.

Without hesitation, the younger man got up from the table and started walking toward us. He was one tough looking character with his muscular build and his chiseled face. It wasn't until he shook our hands and started talking to us that I realized he was more a Teddy Bear than a Grizzly Bear.

"Hi, my name is Chief Petty Officer Collary and it's a real pleasure finally to get to meet you two! I'm probably your biggest fan."

I couldn't help but laugh. "It's more likely, you're our only fan."

Beth quickly spoke up in his defense. "It's better to have one fan than no fans."

"I hate to interrupt this conversation, but I need you two to do me a favor," said the Chief.

"What's that?" asked Beth.

"I need both of you to go over and stand at attention in front of your kitchen sink."

Beth was quite amused with this idea. She had no problem marching over to the kitchen sink and standing at attention for this complete stranger. I was a little more hesitant, but I soon caved in when I saw the smile on my mother's face.

So there we were, the two of us standing at attention in front of our kitchen sink joking around with each other when all of a sudden, Chief Collary started barking out orders. One minute, he says he's our biggest fan, the next minute he thinks he's our Drill Sargent. "Stop your talking and stand up straight! Put your feet together and suck in those stomachs! You two kids are going to have to straighten up if you want to be on my team!"

"Excuse me!" I exclaimed. What the heck is this guy talking about? It was obvious what he said didn't bother Beth, because I could hear her quietly giggling to herself.

Without any further discussion, the Chief then walked over to the kitchen table and stood at attention in front of the older gentleman wearing the Navy uniform.

"Admiral Ryan, the crew is ready for review."

"Very well, Chief Collary!"

Then both Admiral Ryan and my mother stood up from the kitchen table and came walking towards us.

As soon as the Admiral got over to where we were standing, he stood directly in front of Beth.

"Beth Ann Steiner!" said the Admiral. "It is both a pleasure and a privilege for me to award you with the Presidential Medal of Freedom for your heroic acts that helped free the thirty-two hostages, while at the same time you helped recapture the three escaped convicts."

While my mother was handing Admiral Ryan Beth's award, I couldn't help but hear Beth snorting air through her nose in a last ditch effort to try to control her laughter.

The Admiral then took the medal and pinned it on my sister's blouse. He then reached out to shake my sister's hand, but she saluted him instead. He smiled and saluted her back.

Then he came over and stood in front of me. I was so nervous my legs started trembling; I could hardly stand.

"Danny, the President only gave me one medal, so I'm just going to thank you for your heroic actions." Then all of a sudden, the Admiral burst out laughing. "I can't do this!" he said.

The combination of the Admiral not having a medal for me and his outburst of laughter was too much for Beth to bear. The next thing you know; Beth is literally rolling around on the floor laughing her fool head off.

The Admiral looked over at my mother. "Is she alright?"

"She's fine!" said my mother.

The Admiral then reached into his pocket and pulled out a second Presidential Medal of Freedom and pinned it on my shirt and shook my hand. The medal was spectacular. It had a red, white and blue star, surrounded by five golden eagles attached to a beautiful blue ribbon with a sixth golden eagle sewn on to the ribbon.

I was so overcome with joy, it left me speechless.

This would've been the perfect place to end this chapter, but what happened after the award ceremony needs mentioning.

After Beth regained her composure, the Admiral asked all of us to be seated around our kitchen table so we could discuss Beth's and my future.

To start with, we found out Chief Collary was a hero in his own right. It turns out he was a member of one of the most elite commando units in the entire U.S. Navy, SEAL Team Six. He's also a Medal of Honor recipient, which he earned during his second tour in Iraq when he saved three of his fellow SEAL team members during a Top Secret mission.

The reason why I mention these accomplishments, is because Admiral Ryan had just informed me and Beth that we will part of a new Special Ops Team that would include Chief Collary as our team leader.

As I sat there listening to the Admiral explain how Beth and I were going to provide assistance to various government agencies in their time of need, I couldn't help but wonder what had happened to our mother? She's always been like a mother hen when it came to protecting her two little chicks, but today, she just sat there, smiled and nodded her head at everything the Admiral said. She's either been cloned or brainwashed. Either way, Beth and I are headed for the big leagues and we are loving every minute of it.

At the end of the meeting, Admiral Ryan asked if there were any questions.

I raised my hand. "What's the name of our new Special Ops team?"

"There were several names floating around," said the Admiral, "but none of which was any good. So I've come to the conclusion that you and Beth should have the honor of naming your new Special Ops team."

Beth and I both felt since our Super Powers dealt with the use of various types of animals, reptiles and birds, it would only make sense that we name our team after one of the critters. So we both sat there listing one species after another, none of which we could both agree upon. All of a sudden, my mother blurted out the word FROG. The room became silent. I turned and looked at Beth and without saying a word we both smiled.

"Frog Team Five is the perfect name for our new team!" said Beth.

"Beth, what does the five stand for?" I asked.

"It represents the number of members that will be on our team, if you add Mom and Scruffy into the mix."

"Let's make it official," suggested Mom. "Let's vote on it, right here and right now."

"Hold on!" said Beth. She then closed her eyes and within a couple of seconds Scruffy came running into the kitchen and jumped up onto her lap.

Admiral Ryan and Chief Collary were quite impressed with this small demonstration of Beth's powers.

"Danny, is it hard to do what Beth just did?" asked the Admiral.

"It's quite easy if you're lucky enough to be born with the gift."

"Ok, let's get back to business," said the Admiral. "All those who are in favor of Frog Team Five raise your hands."

All four human members immediately raised their hands. Then all eyes were on Scruffy to see his response.

Beth hesitated having Scruffy raise his paw to add to the suspense. When she finally had Scruffy raise his paw, everyone in the room started clapping, except for me. I wasn't impressed. Scruffy had no idea what he was doing. It was just Beth's way of showing off for the Admiral and the Chief.

"I've got to get going," said the Admiral. "One last thing before I go. It's extremely important that the Steiner family gets to know Chief Collary and it's equally as important Chief Collary gets to know the Steiner family. So, I've arranged for the four of you to spend a few days in Orlando, Florida, so you can accomplish this task."

"I'm going to Disney World!" screamed Beth.

The Admiral smiled and then reached into his suitcoat pocket and pulled out four three day passes to Disney World and handed them to Beth. "Beth, don't lose these," said the Admiral.

"Sir, I will guard these passes with my life!" Beth assured him.

The Admiral then looked over at Chief Collary. "Chief Collary! Don't let anything bad happen to these two kids. I look forward to reading about Frog Team Five's adventures. Take care and stay safe."

My mother then escorted the Admiral to our front door.

A couple of weeks ago Beth and I were two average kids enjoying our summer vacation. Today, we are members of an elite Special Ops team. How time flies when you're having fun.

Chapter Nineteen

A Day at the Beach

After three amazing days at Disney World, we decided to spend our fourth and final day at one of Florida's most revered beaches, Daytona Beach.

While my mother sat quietly on the beach reading a romance novel, Bill, formally known as Chief Collary, Beth and I were taking full advantage of some rough surf that had been generated by a tropical storm that had passed out to sea just a few days earlier.

The three of us were swimming close to each other, when all of a sudden Bill got this crazy look in his eyes and declared he was now a sea monster in search for his next meal. He then quickly submerged his entire body and started swimming toward us. Beth ran in one direction, while I swam in the opposite direction. Beth made it to shore alive and unharmed, while I found myself stranded in waist deep sea water wondering if I was going to be the sea monster's next victim.

I was so focused on trying to prevent my own demise, I didn't realize that there was an old lady wading in the water only couple of yards away from where I was standing.

All of a sudden the old lady started screaming at the top of her lungs. It was obvious to me that the sea monster had claimed his first victim. This was the break I needed to swim to shore.

Without any hesitation Bill stood up and immediately started apologizing to the old lady for grabbing her foot. Within a couple of minutes, they were both laughing. Luckily for Bill, the old lady was captivated with his boyish charm, good looks and killer body. He thanked her for being such a good sport before leaving her side.

Bill's face was bright red from embarrassment as he approached us on the beach. Beth and I tried to maintain our composure, but when Bill smiled at us, we both lost it. Together, the three of us just stood there and laughed until Beth almost puked, which only made me and Bill laugh even harder.

As soon as we all settled down, Bill suggested we take a break from swimming and go dry off.

While Bill and I were lying down on the beach working on our tans, Beth sat next to my mother and filled her in on Bill's misfortune.

We couldn't have been on our towels for more than five minutes when all of a sudden a young girl started screaming that her father was drowning. I immediately stood up to see a middle-aged gentleman being carried out to sea by what I can only describe as a rip current.

I turned to look at Bill, but he wasn't there. I turned back around and saw Bill hurdling over numerous sunbathers as he desperately ran toward the water's edge in an attempt to save the gentleman's life. It was at that moment in time that I realized you don't have to have super powers to be a superhero. Bill's willingness to risk his own life to save a complete stranger was proof enough for me that Bill was just as much of a superhero as Beth and I.

I felt a hand grab the back of my leg. I looked down and saw Beth lying on her towel with her eyes closed.

"Danny, there is a pod of dolphins only a short distance from here. Let's get to work!"

I quickly laid back down on my towel in an attempt to connect with one of those dolphins. Within the blink of an eye, Beth and I had completed our transfers and were now swimming as fast as we could toward the last location I remembered seeing the man in trouble swimming.

When we got to where Bill and the man were, we discovered that Bill was struggling to keep the man afloat. The combination of the rip current and the constant wave action was severely hampering Bill's rescue efforts. Luckily for Bill, Beth and I had his back that day.

Bill instantly realized that the two dolphins that came to assist him were me and Beth. "What took you two so long?" Bill laughed as he spoke. "Beth, do me a favor and get in position so this fellow can grab hold of your dorsal fin." Beth slowly moved into position before coming to a full stop, allowing the stranger the perfect opportunity to grab hold of her dorsal fin.

"Sir, do me a favor," said Bill. "Grab hold of this dolphin's dorsal fin and hold on really tight. She will safely tow you all the way back to the beach."

"What about you?" asked the man.

"Don't worry about me," said Bill. "I'll be right behind you."

"Thank you!" said the man as Beth towed him away.

The rip current was no match for Beth's dolphin body. She cut through the water like a hot knife would cut through butter.

It was now time for me to give Bill his ride. So I swam alongside him. He quickly grabbed hold of my dorsal fin. Then with all the power and speed I could muster, I swam as fast as I could towards shore. I really wanted to impress my new Team Leader since it was our first time working together.

We were about halfway back to shore when Bill let go of my dorsal fin and started to swim on his own. He didn't say anything, so I wasn't sure if he was done with me yet. So I decided to follow him in the rest of the way staying submerged the entire time so as not to alarm the other swimmers.

All of sudden, I heard someone running through the water screaming out Bill's name. Since I submerged, I couldn't see what was going above the water, but I was able to hear everything that was said.

"Bill, long time no see!"

"Spike, what are doing out here? Last thing I heard you were stationed in California," said Bill.

"I just got transferred to the USS Abraham Lincoln," said Spike.

"A Navy SEAL attached to an aircraft carrier! How lucky can you get?"

Then I heard Beth's voice. "Danny, I know you're still out there swimming around. I need you to do me a favor and go over to where Bill and that stranger are standing and tell me what they are saying to each other."

Since I was already listening to the conversation that she was asking about, I figured I could wait and tell her later what was said.

Next thing you know, I started experiencing these sharp pains on the left side of my body. It was obvious that Beth was doing something to my human body to get my attention.

Up to now I had never even gave a second thought to how unprotected my human body was during these transfers, but now that Beth had brought it to my attention, I will have to give it some thought in the future.

I realized if I disconnected from this dolphin, there was a good possibility I wouldn't be able to reconnect, so I decided to stay connected and attempt to reason with Beth by talking to her.

"Beth, what are you doing to me?"

"What are you talking about?" asked Beth. "I'm just standing here watching Bill talk to some stranger. Why do you ask?"

"I was just experiencing a whole lot of pain on the left side of my body. It's funny how it stopped the second I started to talk to you."

"If you had only answered my question when I asked it, I wouldn't have had to punish you by digging my jagged toenails into your side."

"Beth, you never cease to amaze me. I will get you the information you desire under one condition; you keep your nasty feet to yourself."

"Danny, I'll give you ten minutes. If at the end of that ten minutes you still haven't gotten back to me, I will be forced to release a real live crab down the back of your bathing suit. How does that sound?"

"I must admit that sounds like something you would do."

Knowing that Beth was most likely already searching the beach for the largest crab possible, I wasted no time getting back listening to Bill's and Spike's conversation.

"Spike, you finding me on this beach today wasn't an accident, was it?"

"No, it wasn't," said Spike. "I have orders from Admiral Ryan to bring you and your Frog Team Five members back to the Abraham Lincoln with me."

"Why does Admiral Ryan want Frog Team Five onboard the USS Abraham Lincoln?" asked Bill.

"He didn't tell me and I sure didn't ask. So if you could round up your men, I would really appreciate it, because there is boat load of SEALs on their way here to extract you and your crew from this beach."

"Just so you're aware, other than myself, there are no men assigned to Frog Team Five. My entire crew is made up of two kids, their mother and their pet dog."

Spike started laughing. "Bill, you always were the joker of the group. If that was the case, why would the Admiral send me out here to extract you and your team?"

"All I can tell you is the two kids that make up the heart of Frog Team Five are very talented. They have abilities you couldn't even imagine. I have seen them in action and what I saw was only the tip of the iceberg. There is nothing these kids can't do when they put minds to it."

"I can't wait to meet them," said Spike.

Shortly after Bill's and Spike's conversation ended, I disconnected from my host dolphin so I could inform my mother and Beth about the SEALs' plans to extract us from the beach and bring us onboard the US aircraft carrier the Abraham Lincoln.

It only took the SEALs about five minutes to get us and our belongings onboard their hovercraft, once they arrived at the beach. Then at a very high rate of speed, we headed back out to sea to rendezvous with the USS Abraham Lincoln.

Luckily for me, Beth never found a crab that day, because I exceeded the amount of time that she had allotted me.

Chapter Twenty

The Beginning of a Long Voyage

W e had been underway onboard the Seals' high-speed hovercraft for only a short time when I spotted several US Navy warships just off our port bow.

Having little to no knowledge of US naval vessels, I turned to Bill for some answers. "Bill, I thought we were only going onboard one naval vessel. I count at least eight."

"Danny, all those ships you see over there are part of a battle group. The only one we're interested in is that gigantic one located in the very middle of the pack, the USS Abraham Lincoln."

"Wow!" said Beth. "That is one massive ship!"

"Yes, she is Beth," said Bill. "She's twenty-four stories tall, three football fields long, and she weighs in excess of one hundred thousand tons."

"Bill, how is it you know so much about aircraft carriers?" I asked.

"Before I became a SEAL Team member, I was attached to an aircraft carrier named the USS Nimitz for four years. She was an older version of the Abraham Lincoln, but very similar in design."

As we got closer to the naval war ships, I found myself mesmerized by their majestic beauty. Each ship was beautiful in its own way, but it was the USS Abraham Lincoln that stood out from all the rest. It wasn't just because of her immense size. It was more than just that. I've never seen the Great Wall of China, the Pyramids of Giza or even the Sphinx, but I can't even imagine anything more spectacular on this entire planet than what I saw that day when I got my first close-up look at the USS Abraham Lincoln in all her glory. The only word that even comes close to describing what I experienced that day is breathtaking.

As the SEALs slowly maneuvered their hovercraft alongside the USS Abraham Lincoln, I observed a makeshift stairway coming down the side of the huge ship. On that stairway stood several sailors waiting to assist us.

As soon as we got onboard, we met up with the second in command, or in naval terms, the Executive Officer. After a quick round of handshakes and introductions, we were escorted up to the bridge so we could meet with the commanding officer of the USS Abraham Lincoln, Capt. James Hathaway.

The interior of the aircraft carrier was just as massive as the outside. There were doorways, hallways, stairwells, hatchways, you name it, they had it. I felt like a little tiny mouse who had just been let loose inside this gigantic maze.

It took us nearly twenty minutes before we arrived at the door that led on to the bridge. Just outside of that door, stood a Marine guard.

Beth was just about to make one of her trademark comments when my mother placed her hand over Beth's mouth.

The Marine saluted the Executive Officer as he held the door open for all of us to enter.

Capt. James Hathaway, a chubby, bald-headed fellow whose smile lit up the room, came over to greet us the second we walked on to the bridge.

"Welcome aboard the USS Abraham Lincoln," said Captain Hathaway. "It's a real pleasure to have the four of you onboard my ship."

The captain stood in front of Bill first and shook his hand. "It's a real honor finally to get to meet you, Chief Collary," said Capt. Hathaway. "It's not every day you get to meet a Medal of Honor recipient."

"Thank you, Captain Hathaway. It's a pleasure to meet you too, sir," said Bill.

The Captain then moved over and stood in front of my mother and shook her hand. "Welcome aboard, Mrs. Steiner," said the Captain. "I bet you never expected to be onboard a United States aircraft carrier when you signed up to be a full-time member of Frog Team Five."

"Nope, I definitely didn't see this coming," said Mom.

"Mrs. Steiner, how do feel about being on my aircraft carrier?" asked the Captain.

"It sure beats housework!"

"I like the way you think Mrs. Steiner!" said the Captain.

Captain Hathaway then came over and stood in front of me and Beth. "I thought you two would be bigger based on everything I read about you."

Beth looked up at Captain Hathaway and said, "It's not always the big dogs you have to fear in life. It's those little tiny ones that you ignore that end up gnawing your ankles when you're not paying attention."

The captain smiled at Beth. "So you're telling me you are a dangerous individual."

"Let's just say there are three hardened criminals sitting behind bars right this second who wish they had never seen the likes of me and one of my big furry friends," said Beth.

The Captain laughed. He then turned and looked over at me. "I'm guessing your little sister is a handful to work with."

"A handful? It's more like a truck full. Sometimes I fear her more than I fear the villains I'm up against."

Beth just stood there with a big smile on her face nodding her head in agreement.

Bill interrupted. "Sir, what is the reason for bringing us on board the USS Abraham Lincoln at this time?"

"Two days ago I received orders from the Secretary of the Navy to make preparations to get the USS Abraham Lincoln underway by noon today. Those orders also stated that I would have two Special Operations Teams onboard prior to our departure. The two teams mentioned in my orders were SEAL Team Six and Frog Team Five. Yesterday, SEAL Team Six arrived onboard, and now today Frog Team Five has arrived, completing my pre-underway requirements. Now there is nothing preventing us from getting underway."

"Where are we going?" asked Beth.

"Since my orders were Top Secret all I can tell you is we are going to the continent of Africa," said the Captain.

"Lions, tigers and bears, OH MY!" declared Beth.

"Beth!" I said. "There are no tigers or bears living in the wild in Africa."

"Ok Danny! Lions, hippos, elephants, giraffes, and a whole lot more, OH MY!" said Beth.

We all laughed at Beth's comment.

"Captain Hathaway, what are the sleeping arrangements when it comes to Frog Team Five?" asked Bill.

"During our transit across the Atlantic Ocean, Bill, you will be, sharing one stateroom with Danny, and Mrs. Steiner, you will be sharing your stateroom with Beth and Scruffy."

"SCUFFY!" screamed Beth. "Where's my baby?"

"Right now we're keeping him down in one of the kennels where we keep all our other dogs. I will have him brought up to your stateroom this evening before you go to bed."

"Thank you!" said Beth. She could hardly contain herself with this new reality.

"I have a question?" asked Mom. "What are we supposed to wear while we are onboard the USS Abraham Lincoln?"

"I arranged to have a couple of my personnel who work in the Uniform Department to come to your staterooms after dinner tonight and fit all four of you with brand new uniforms.

"Now, if there are no further questions, it's time to get this show on the road," said Captain Hathaway.

Silence then followed.

"Officer of the Deck, inform the battle group that the package has arrived onboard and its time to get underway. Helmsman, come left to new course one two zero and engines all ahead full."

"Aye, aye sir!" said the young man steering the ship.

Beth and I quickly ran over to one of the many windows that surrounded the bridge. From where we stood, we were able to witness the entire battle group getting underway. It was amazing to watch all these giant warships turn in unison.

"I hope you've enjoyed reading my story as much as I enjoyed writing it."

Yours Truly Danny Steiner.